70 SANDUNE'S WAY

By Mercia Macdonald

TABLE OF CONTENTS:

'In memory of my Mum, Diana, and my Dad Roy Paine'

PREFACE:

It was the late 60's and early **70's and June's way** of life was the way that most young girls go when they are coming of age.

She was at the age when boundaries are tested, the meaning of freedom explored, and the values she had grown up with, questioned.

Together with her friends, the moral and ethical issues of their situation as white South Africans became more complicated and the problem of loyalties, because of peer pressure had to be uneasily addressed.

The complex mixture of South African politics, religion and the drug culture, did not help June's failing view on life.

It was only when she experienced a dynamic encounter with God that everything seemed to make sense at last.

CHAPTER 1

The sand dune cast a long shadow across the soft sand as the surfer invited June to sit down next to him. She submitted, after all she had enjoyed his attentions. He had said, 'lets go for a walk and get to know each other.' Why he wanted to get to know 'little' her was a mystery that deserved finding out. This was where he had led her... to a secluded spot behind a big sand dune. He had been one of those overfriendly teenagers who had accepted her into the group even though she was a bit of a misfit and so much younger than the others, but oh! how important it was for her to feel included.

The hot sand pillowed her long skinny legs as she awkwardly settled down beside him. He reclined next to her and she could feel his warm breath on her neck as he began to caress her body. His attentions became suddenly stifling, and she did her best to hide her alarm. Blind innocence had led her to this place and it was her own fault. How silly to think that the young man only wanted her friendship, and yet she felt an element of childish gratification that she was even remotely desirable, especially since she was way out of his league in experience and age. A sudden feeling of flight overwhelmed her. It was stronger than the initial curiosity that had crept up on her in the first place. Quite without any warning, she jumped to her feet, murmuring beneath her breath something that was hardly audible.

She bolted around the edge of the grassy sand dune like a young filly loosed from her tack. Down towards the sea she dashed. A sense of freedom overcame her. Her heart was thumping violently in her chest, and she felt mildly violated by what had just taken place. Whatever his intentions were, and in her childish mind, they were hard to interpret, she resolved to avoid any such advances again. She was keen to get away and ran until quite out of breath, putting the unpleasant occurrence behind her.

Her gait soon slowed down to a saunter along the beach. She brushed her hair away from her face hoping that the dark thoughts would go too, and frowned pensively, drawing lines in the shiny wet sand with her toes. The sun was shining in her face yet in the distance she could see a familiar figure walking towards her.

With a sigh of relief she quickened her steps towards the approaching silhouette . Greeting him with a shy smile, her hair brushed against his cheek. Bobby wondered what he had done to earn such a warm greeting. Not sure how to interpret the moment, he presented June with a fish. She laughed and stepped backwards to inspect the hard earned prize and then she affectionately tugged at his shirt. He started talking about Gremmies pier and how it was the best place in the world to fish. June giggled nervously and she wound her arm tightly around his, so that he could not escape.

Although Bob was only thirteen, he had already been viewed by the other boys as a loner, who would rather fish than surf. The two loners had met a few months before. June, being lonely because she had been introduced to a new and foreign country, had finally found a friend in the young boy who liked fishing. In their child like way they had grown attached to one another, and had even held hands, sharing their innermost thoughts.

But of late, his affections had turned elsewhere, and the infatuation had faded as the love of a boy inevitably does. At this particular moment though, all those conflicting emotions were put on hold and the relief of meeting a friend, made her bold and forgiving in the light of the embarrassing moment which had just occurred. Bobby was never to know, and would have been indifferent, anyway, to the backdrop of this sudden outburst of reawakened friendship, which, frankly caused him to become a little apprehensive. They soon parted, awkwardly aware of their youthful inexperience in dealing with the conflicting feelings connected with a strained relationship.

CHAPTER 2

'I think, therefore I am'
Moody Blues 1969

She weaved her way through the buildings towards her home and looked up at the eleventh floor where her mother often kept watch. It was supper time, and as usual there she was, at her watch tower scanning the surface below her, like a hawk from its lofty heights. Her mother proceeded to wave at her and was relieved to see her child appear from the shadows of the high rise buildings. It always reminded the older woman of a small insect emerging from the confines of a rock bed.

A plate of hot food was placed lovingly on the table as June entered more quietly than usual. She closed the door gently behind her and felt a bit unworthy of the tender care that was lavished upon her every afternoon without fail. In the meantime, Mother pottered around in the kitchen.

'So, how was your day?' She asked, casually, although already sensing something unusual had happened. June hesitated.

'It was ok'. Came the quiet answer, and then without warning, she launched into a fairly accurate account of her version of the day's happenings, avoiding the occurrence on the beach with the amorous young man.

'I messed around with Bob, he caught a couple of fish down at the Gremmies Pier. Good to see him, I think I popped a few buttons off his shirt again.... I guess I am kind of rough with him' suddenly she was chatting rather too cheerfully, hardly taking a breath between sentences, which caused her mother to be even more suspicious. She laughed and her mother responded with an approving grunt and left it at that. June had nothing more to say, and wolfed down her food, withdrawing promptly to her bedroom.

Her mother had used the twelve year old's room as a means to express her creative side. Giving it a typical 60's look, with matching curtains and bedcover, printed with bold colourful patterns, which she felt, suited a young, growing girl.

It was a sun facing room .... Cheerful and bright, was what it was meant to be and at that moment, anything of that nature was welcomed, as she peered timidly in the mirror.

She was not sure what to make of her reflection. How to cope with the changes in her body was a mystery to her. Her 'training' bra was uncomfortable and the fact that her nose was getting bigger was of special concern to her. Her freckles stood starkly out on her face, and the sunburn didn't help the matter at hand.

She knew she couldn't avoid the bright sunshine, because there was a need to be accepted by the beach kids. That meant stripping off and sunbathing. To sit in the shade and remain fair of skin was not viewed as cool at all. It was important, even necessary to get a tan, even if it meant that it would darken her freckles even more. But then again, she had resigned herself to the fact that nobody seemed to want to be her friend anyway, because she was different,.... *freckly with a strange accent*. She had been different in her last home as well. In Canada, she was viewed as .... *freckly with a strange accent* and to add to her grief, she had acquired a nickname....'strawberry face'. That was a good enough reason to leave Canada. England had

5

been a similar experience, this was where the family had settled before immigrating to Canada.... there she was seen as *freckly with a strange accent.* The only difference was, that it had been her long platted hair which had been a highlight for the bullies, who incessantly pulled it without mercy, everyday, after school... terrible twins, who harassed the living day lights out of her.

Only in Kenya was there a connection. The memories of her first home were still vivid in her mind. Those idyllic golden days growing up in the house that her Dad had built, surrounded by giant leopard and jacaranda trees, had been followed by that fateful day which she so well remembered. The day they had to leave all that was dear to them. It was at the train station as they were saying goodbye to their many friends and relatives, that she first ever saw her mother cry. Then only did it hit home that they would never return. June often wondered why her Dad was in such a hurry to leave Kenya. It seemed such an urgent thing to do. She only knew that the country had been granted its independence and that her dad, two decades before, had been part of the British Police Force that had occupied the country to keep the Mau-Mau uprising at bay. The[i] new president had been in prison for many years, because of his involvement in the Mau-Mau rebellion. This must've been the reason for their sudden flight out of the country. After this her father insisted that they should never return because it would 'break their hearts'

She forced her thoughts to return to the subject at hand. Staring reluctantly at her skinny, boyish body she could not imagine growing up into something a little more pleasing to the eye. Never mind that, what was the purpose for her very existence? 'Who am *I*?' she muttered under her breath, gazing at the face staring back at her. Suddenly a strange, new sensation gripped her, the feeling of existence....self realization...what could it all mean? . She began to brush her hair hoping that as she did so she would brush away such deep thoughts.

A cup of hot chocolate was always the answer to all her problems and her mother was always faithful with such a task. This evening was no different.

CHAPTER 3

'Oh I get by with a little help from my friends'
Joe Cocker 1969

'Meet me in the park after school' whispered the girl, sitting at the opposite side of the classroom, as she menacingly waved her fist at June. Trouble had followed her around in every school. Being a magnet for bullies was not pleasant, and here she was once more face to face with the school bully, who gave her a couple of slaps and called her a 'bleddy rooi neck' and sent her home with a ripped dress, while all the school kids looked on with glee. Tearfully, June explained her dilemma to her dad who then took great lengths in demonstrating how she should deal with the situation.

'What you do' said her Dad with child like zeal

'is pretend you are retreating in fear, saying "no!, no! don't hurt me" then, when the bully lets down her guard, give her one giant slug and run for it!'. June looked blankly at her dad as he positioned himself like a boxer, and demonstrated his punches.

She was not impressed with his advice. All she could think of, was how her dad had missed his calling as a boxer or possibly a second class actor. He obviously wasn't taking it seriously. She gave him a weak smile and retired to her room to think about the problem more realistically. The realistic thing to do, was not to attend school the next day but after getting told off by her mother, who also seemed oblivious to the crisis at hand, June bravely returned to school. She then, had to appear before the headmaster who was very angry at the whole affair and gave her and her enemy detention for a week. She only wished that her big sister Mandy would show some interest in her problem at hand. In Canada when a 'kid' was out to get her, Mandy would invariably come to the rescue. Her pretty sister's presence was so tangible, always at the right time, just when June had got herself into some fix or other. No-one would touch little sister when big sister was around. But those days were over. Mandy was too taken up with her own interests, namely her new boyfriend, Tommy.

Hence, it was important to find some kindred spirits to hook up with. It was a matter of the survival of the fittest, and June knew that she wasn't very fit. She knew she had some serious growing up to do. What could be done to secure this objective?

It eventually materialised in the form of a small, Jewish girl of the same age. Her name was Rachel. She was cute and popular to the point of being virtually the school mascot. If you were seen with Rachel then you were cut above the rest. Fortunately Rachel felt the same way about June. Perhaps what brought them together was the fact that they both felt a little different from the rest. The friendship was convenient and secured a bit of leverage during her early school days in this strange, new country, and to June, a strange country it was indeed. This was not the Africa that she remembered in her childhood, with its beautiful skies and gentle rustling of the tree tops, this was inner city Durban, South Africa, with the biggest natural harbour in Africa and all the problems that go with such a setting.

The bullying continued for June into high school, except that the term *bully* could no longer be used lightly. They had now evolved into literal 'heavy weights' while June had secured, as well as Rachel, a set of friends that could only be seen as light weights, even such a word could not correctly describe her four friends, a more motley group of waifs could not be found anywhere.

Their one and only means of salvation from the miserable fate awaiting them, came in the form of friend number five, Sammy, the Karate expert! Hence, they all leaned heavily on her claim to a black belt. Unfortunately there was always the temptation to become overconfident, because of Sammy's presence. Friend number one, Celeste, found it her duty to shout threats across the school grounds at the enemy.

'You fat bitches, only a mother could love you!' she would yell at the top of her voice. June would giggle nervously at her side, while Sammy slept soundly on Celeste's shoulder on the other side. She would not admit it out loud, but June had a horrible feeling that something awful was going to happen when Sam wasn't around, and so Sam was dragged everywhere with the four for security reasons. But one afternoon, while June and Celeste were on their way home and sitting casually on the crowded bus, the dreaded moment arrived. There in front of them stood the enemy. Her raven black hair straddled her potted, pale face. Her eyes had no colour in them and could only be described as pitch black pupils. She looked like she had just stepped out of a coffin and was determined to bring death to the race of brunette girls. Suddenly Celeste had nothing to say but was completely dumbstruck in her all pervading presence.

'Your not so mouthy now are you bitch?' said the opponent under her breath, as she loomed over the two girls like a black threatening cloud. Celeste looked around at June for support, not sure who was being addressed with such vengeance, but clearly hoping that it was not herself. She looked out of the window, dumbstruck, her face losing colour rapidly.   Then without any warning June received a clout across the head that made her ears ring, while Celeste continued to peer out of the window....

* * *

'What happened to you?' it was Bobby enquiring. All the school boys had got onto the bus on the routine journey home from school. June was too traumatised to answer, and wondered why he had asked the question, she guessed that the bloodshot eyes from crying and her dishevelled hair must have been a giveaway. She didn't feel like talking about it, especially to him, he always seemed to be there when something horrible had happened, and now it was no longer a novelty.

Anyway, the way the boys looked, left much to be desired. Their shirts were always hanging out and their ties carelessly shoved in their back pockets. 'If anyone looked dishevelled it was them', thought June as she peered around the bus resentfully. All they could ever talk about was the surf, the only time they even showed an inkling of interest in the girls was when there was an Easterly wind blowing, and then that was just a *bumma* for them. Her thoughts began to darken as she watched them jump enthusiastically off the bus straight onto the beach front. All this did not stop her, though, from reaching into her school bag and pulling out a small mirror to view the damages done to her. Yes, it *was* bad after all. She supposed that, actually, on second thoughts, it was quite decent of Bobby to even ask after her well being

The next day, word had got around that there had been a brawl on the bus. Overnight Celeste had changed completely, and had become quite docile, even losing confidence in her best friend Sammy. She had

11

resorted to silence, and suddenly June became the despised target. Resignedly, June had decided that if she was going to die, she would accept it with grace. She also had lost faith in the loyalty of her friends. She made her way to the tuck shop at lunchtime with no backup. Inevitably, there to meet her was the dreaded girl with the raven black hair and her faithful followers.

Quivering with fear, June began to count every breath, aware that the next breath could be the last. The black eyed girl snarled at her, bearing a row of crooked teeth. To June's relief, the dreadful moment was delayed, as a pretty senior prefect with a long flaxen ponytail glided up to the enemy and tapped her on the shoulder.

'What the hell do you think you are doing picking on girls that are half your size!' She exclaimed, her beautiful smooth brow faintly creasing with irritation.

'Ok, Ok, I'll leave her alone, that's cool, I'm out of here.' Came the answer. The raven haired girl raised her hands in a manner of surrender. Glaring at her for a minute, the senior twirled gracefully on her toes to go. Without warning and as sudden as a predator to the kill, the enemy grabbed the pretty prefect by the pony tail and spun her around and within a split second the two were locked together, and like a spinning wheel, all June could see, was a blur of school colours, and chunks of black and golden hair flying all around the room. School girls ran in every direction to avoid being caught in the cross fire of blows.

'What have I done to bring this onto myself' thought June, as the tatty school girls presented themselves before the head mistress. She looked around at her friends and enemies and the beautiful prefect who was worse for wear after the ordeal and it dawned upon her that someone was missing. It was Rachel, where was her little friend?

12

Perhaps she had made herself scarce during the battle that had ensued. June could not blame her for that. Suddenly, she felt hot breath on her back and turned around to see who was behind her. Rachel looked up at her apologetically and shivered slightly. The little wretch, had conveniently tucked herself away behind June's bigger frame. They glanced at each other and then began to giggle nervously. There had been a funny side to the episode after all.

CHAPTER 4

"Sitting on the Dock of the Bay watching the tide roll away"
Small faces 1965

'There is a certain resilience about youth, you'll be ok', reflected Dad philosophically, as he folded up his newspaper and retired to the bedroom.

'Well, I should just be satisfied that my dad is willing to hear about my daily traumas, even if I didn't tell him the whole story, in case he gave me another demonstration of how to cope with the incident in hind sight.' she thought, and felt a little better for disclosing half the story to him.

There was only one way to move on and that was to get her shorts on and call on her friend, Barbara, who had a rope. The rope was very useful for climbing over walls and jumping on trains down at the docks, where they had made it a habit to ride along the harbour, waving at the ships, as the great, bulky sea vessels embarked on their journey out to sea. Often they would hoist themselves up on a wall and watch the sun set over the sea. Down below them, beyond the wall, was a very large hostel, where all the black labourers would gather every evening.   [ii]Hundreds of African men would sit around fires, smoking and chatting in Zulu. On this particular evening, the pungent smell of tobacco, caught June in the throat. She coughed loudly and the men spotted the two of them on the wall. White pearly teeth against a canvas of black faces glimmered in the twilight, as the Africans laughed heartily at the sight of the two tomboys sitting on the wall with their rope. June wondered why they were never seen on the beach or on the streets. They were all squashed in a confined space, which didn't seem to be very comfortable for them. She knew enough to realize that they had left their families in the rural areas, to come to the city to find work but she could not understand why they would want to work under such hard conditions. It was all so unreasonable. Yet they seemed happy enough, as they drank their homemade Juba brew.

***

'Darling, darling' you must get up. Don't worry everything is alright' mother tried to speak calmly but June could sense the anxiety in her voice. Sleepily she arose and her mother helped her into her dressing gown and guided her out of the flat. Her Dad and her big sister, Mandy, followed close on their heels along the corridor to the lift where everyone was congregating. The frightened tenants seemed agitated as they made their way down the staircase. June leaned against the wall, aware now of what the problem was, there had been an earth tremor and the building was still wavering a bit. All the tenants were doing their best not to panic but they could not help but feel confused about what to do. A boy was standing against the opposite wall with his dad, both father and son lived together in the studio flat down the corridor from June's flat. Still groggy from sleep, he and his dad had vacated the studio reluctantly. The boy stood in the shadows with a sleepy expression and glanced at June. His lips creased into half a smile. She had seen him on the beach and learned that his name was Kenny, 'little Kenny' he was often called. At last the building was vacated and the pyjama clad crowd sat around outside the looming, high rise block of flats, waiting for the earth to tremor again, and after awhile they all retired to bed, not sure of what would follow.   Nothing did follow.

It was the next evening that June found herself in the lift with Kenny's dad.   As the door of the lift opened on the eleventh floor, there to meet them was a very wet surfer boy who was trying to get into his flat. Ken's surfboard was leaning against the wall and he was frantically trying to unlock the door.

'Where were you today!' his dad exclaimed. Ken looked vacantly at his dad.

'What do you mean, I was at school of course,' he answered curtly.

'No you weren't, I was there and you were not at school' came his dad's adamant reply. There was silence for a moment, as Ken scrambled for an excuse.

'Oh yeh, it was parent's day today, wow, I forgot about that.' He cowered a little at being discovered

16

playing truant from school. His voice tapered off a little, but then with renewed gusto, he answered his dad,

'Ah Dad there was a Westerly today, the surf was up, I couldn't help it the waves were calling me'

June caught Ken's eye just before she disappeared around the corner. He didn't seem too bothered that his Dad had turned up at his school for parent's day only to find that his surly son was out surfing. As she walked down the corridor she could still hear his dad chiding him half heartedly. She felt mildly amused yet puzzled at the relationship between father and son, they were like two ships passing in the night, neither the one knew what the other was doing, but she had to give his dad his due, he had tried to connect with his son by turning up at parent's day.

CHAPTER 5

"Down by the sea, oh yeh, on a blanket with my
baby....that's where I'll be"
The drifters 1964

The best thing about school was the school holidays and the lazy mornings. In her semiconscious state she could hear her mother's voice, droning on in back ground about all the things that needed to be done, while she was at work and to confirm that it wasn't all a bad dream, June eventually awoke to a list of chores, scribbled on a scrap of paper, by the side of her bed. The sun boldly stared at her, like a big yellow disapproving face, as if to say 'wake up you lazy thing!' It penetrated through the curtains, aggressively throwing as much heat on her as possible for so early in the morning.

As she propped herself up sleepily, she could see her reflection in the mirror, her hair, now, had natural highlights from the sun and at last her skin had acquired a golden tone which helped her to fit in with the others. Fortunately her nose had settled down to an acceptable size and had just a little bit of an arch to it, the current challenge was, how to keep it from becoming sunburnt and scabby. The grazes on her knees were also in the process of healing, since she had explained to Barbara, that she didn't want to be a tom boy anymore, but that it was time to grow up and look pretty. Just a bit of makeup would suffice she decided as she stumbled out of bed, and thought for awhile about what would be the best things to wear on this already very hot day.

Her thoughts were distracted by the sight of her Bible lying unopened by her bedside. She had resolved to make a point of reading it, since she had returned the year before from a camp which her mother had bundled her off to. She did not hesitate to ask why she had to be packed off to camp. Her mother's answer was simple and to the point, 'to keep you off the streets.' And that was that, no more arguments.

It had been a hot and humid time. The camp ground was a few yards from the beach. Each evening the young campers met around a big fire, and sang Christian songs followed by a short word from the Bible.

One afternoon, June escaped to a quiet spot on the back step of the camp's kitchen. She sat down to enjoy her afternoon meal in the shade, relieved that the fatigue that she was suffering from seemed to be fading. Her sunburnt shoulders were beginning to hurt, when, without invitation, somebody came and sat with her on the step. It was a convenient distraction from the pain and she didn't mind the intrusion. Who was she to mind? After all a thirteen year old couldn't really protest, especially since it was one of the senior young people at the camp. The stranger did not mince his words, he just came right out with it.

[iii]"Would you like to know Jesus Christ?" he asked.

With a mouthful of food, June found it difficult to answer him. But this did not dissuade him from his mission. While she chewed her food, and gestured with her knife and fork, he began to pray for her and then expected her to repeat words after him. She guessed he was not aware that her mother had taught her not to talk with her mouth full, nevertheless, to please him and also to make sure of his prompt departure, she submitted to his wishes. Eventually, to June's relief the stranger left. She was puzzled at what had just

19

occurred, and was not sure what should be done from that moment on. Terms such as sin, forgiveness, Jesus and Saviour, were all new to her. She couldn't quite grasp it all, but in an odd sort of way she felt that she had done something quite honourable.

So, now here was the Bible lying forlornly next to her bed. She had failed to fulfil her resolution up till then. It was all too much of a chore, and anyway, there was no time for that.

Wandering down to the beach, she saw from a distance her new friends sitting on the wall, overlooking the sea. The little loner felt like she belonged at last. This was more important to her than anything else.

***

'There's some good waves!' shouted one of the lads to his mates as they waxed their surf boards and dashed into the sea, skimming along the surface of the foam, ducking under the first wave to meet the next wave eagerly.

The gaggle of girls stretched out on the sand, showing off their hard earned tans which they were nurturing with sun tan oil every so often. They displayed themselves glamorously, while June sat awkwardly, and fully clad..that is in her vest and shorts. It was a bit like being a 'thorn amongst the roses' observed the freckled creature, but she couldn't help it, until her body began to show some signs of acceptable curves, the arrangement stood.

An amateur photographer who had taken her down to the gremmies pier had felt differently though and on showing her the successful snaps that he had taken of her, had then gone on to show them to a circle of other photographers who had tried to persuade her to

have some more pictures taken, but this time in a studio with only her bikini on. She felt too embarrassed to do that, not because she didn't want to but because she perceived her body as not perfect enough.

She took out a cigarette and lit it, as she sat down boyishly, next to her look alike Barbie doll friends.

'Wanna smoke?' she asked the one closest to her. She knew that all her cigarettes would be gone within a matter of minutes if she offered them around, 'but hey' she thought, 'that's the price you have to pay to be accepted'.

'What are we doing tonight?' asked Annie. June wasn't sure whether it was her being addressed or not. Most often it wasn't her, as she still had the nagging feeling that she hadn't actually been fully accepted into the group, She felt that they were 'kinda tolerating' her, as she put it. She sat quietly smoking, while the girls discussed the day's happenings.

Smoking had become a necessary evil, to be socially accepted. Celeste had taught her well. It was the day that, on the spur of the moment, they had skipped the idea of going to school and instead ended up at Celeste's place and that is where June had her legs shaved for the very first time. Celeste was an expert at things like that and at the same time, she taught June some important social skills, like how to smoke a cigarette in a lady like fashion and how to apply makeup. So, now she did all those things and did them very well.

The boys took the lead on deciding what was next on the schedule for the day, as they stumbled out of the surf, blue and shivering, sniffing and snorting salt water all over the girls. They protested with squeals of delight, sort of saying 'don't!.. we love it.'

It was decided that football would be the afternoon activity, continuing into the evening. This was June's favourite pastime and she loved it when they all congregated in the field together, as that was what the holidays were all about... football and surfing. As the day went on, two groups routinely formed, those that could *really* play football and those who were just fooling around.

By the time it was dusk most of the girls retreated to the stands to watch the boys, especially Luke who was a cut above the others in beauty. His blonde hair flapped around his face as he strided past the girls with his teeshirt hooked to his baggies, displaying his sinewy body. Like a Palamino pony bounding past, he seemed unaware that all eyes were on him.

'I'd do anything for him' muttered Lucy, under her breath, June was not sure whether Lucy was actually sharing the thought with her or not, as Lucy's heavily lashed eyes were fixed on him and him alone. He was without doubt the darling of the football field. He was popular with the lads because he played a good game of football, and most girls would have done anything to spend the night with him. Flippantly, June was tempted to agree with Lucy, but after glancing at her pained expression she felt that the less said on the subject the better.

'Hey, who's *pad* should we go to tonight?' It was Jay's voice. Lately the group had been taking turns at using their homes as a place to hang out. The poor host was expected to supply the cigarettes, drinks, snacks and entertainment for the night, and the parents of such were not impressed with the new routine. There was a weak response from everyone. June was still pondering Lucy's last words, when her thoughts were interrupted by the sudden silence and realized that all eyes were intently upon her.

'You haven't had a turn' exclaimed Jay as he shoved his finger in June's face. Without much warning he declared to all, that the gang would meet at June's place that night. The girl tried to protest but found herself speechless. What would her mum and dad think of an invasion such as this taking place in their home. She was envisioning at least twenty five of them expecting cigarettes, cool drinks and entertainment on the house.

On the contrary, and much to the young hostess's surprise, her family seemed delighted with the idea, and although her dad did not comment, he didn't seem too perturbed with the sudden invasion of teenagers.. One by one they arrived and each time her dad flipped his paper back to see who it was, he was greeted by another goofy footed youngster who ambled through to June's half lit bedroom. Soon they were spilling out into the lounge and her mother was compelled to entertain them around the table with a game of cards and Cluedo. Now and again June looked into the lounge apologetically, but soon relaxed after assuring herself that her mother was having a whale of a time.

'What have we got here?' exclaimed Jay as he peered at June's wardrobe full of clothes. It was a built in wardrobe and could easily hold a full grown man. Jay disguised his unhealthy interest in June's clothes by suggesting a game.

'This is how it's played' said he, as he squeezed inside the cupboard. 'When one of the gang arrives, ask them what they think of me . I will be right here' he pointed at himself with a reassuring gesture and flexed his large muscles. Hesitating a moment to emphasize his point, he continued,

'I will be taking note of *everything* that is said about me.' He snickered slyly and pulled the cupboard door shut on himself. It did not take a genius to work out what the consequence of such a game would be. Possibly the end of life for a poor uninformed soul who spoke too freely about his or her true feelings concerning the queer young Jay.

June was just as puzzled as all the others but the mischievious pranksters were ready for a bit of fun, at the expense of the unexpecting individual who was going to be thrust upon with the question of his opinion concerning the well built bully hiding among June's clothes, whose temperament, at the best of times was to say the least, volatile.

It did not take long for a poor unsuspecting boy to caper casually into the room before the risky question was fired. It was little Ken who became the unsuspecting victim.

'Hey Kenny, what do you think of Jay Van der Merwe?' piped up Mouse, who was called Mouse because of his size.

'Jay?' came the reply, a tense silence ensued, followed by a nervous chuckle. All faces were intently turned in his direction, Ken's dreamy, green eyes, dreamy because he always seemed half asleep, floated from one person to the other. He flicked his thumb at the cupboard, giving an enquiring signal of Jay's where-abouts. June nodded and gestured towards the cupboard. 'I think....' reckoned Ken cautiously, his voice suddenly became a whisper

'...what's the dick head doing in there?....' his voice gained volume....

'He's quite a cool guy'.

Jay could only hear the tail end of the reply. The humoured audience waited for the reaction. Jay's plan had been to jump out of the cupboard and attack his assailant but the game had been sabotaged by Ken's diplomatic response. What could he do now but sit amongst June's clothes and wait until everyone had lost interest in him. After awhile the cupboard door creaked opened and sheepishly Jay crept out, as if it was normal to spend the evening crouched in a dark corner of a girl's wardrobe. He nodded at Ken casually and made himself scarce for the rest of the night.

'Hey June, lets look at your music' said Bugsy enthusiastically. He began to sift through her meagre collection of LPs. LPs were expensive, and June had to be particularly selective of her choice of music, so that it was accepted by her friends but had an element of individuality as well. The balance was hard to find, especially since she was so young and was a novice at such things.

He twirled his cigarette between his fingers, and then accidentally dropped it onto the carpet. There was a smell of burning as the carpet was left with a small singed patch. He scooped it up and with one movement placed it between his lips again and resumed what he was doing. Flipping Bob Dylan, Led Zeppelin, and Spooky Tooth to one side, his eyes fell on one that was unfamiliar to him.

'How did that get into my collection?' grimaced June, embarrassed that he had found one of her mum's albums tucked away in the small pile. She had to confess to herself that she secretly enjoyed listening to the 'Goon Show'..but there was no way that she could tell Bugsy. She watched his reaction with interest. His cigarette, now a mere stub, hung limply from the side of his mouth, and his one eye was closed against the smoke. A look of curiosity was eclipsed by a hint of approval and he passed the disc to June, and nodded. Obediently, she placed it on the turntable and breathed a sigh of relief. It crackled into the sounds of the 50's. Comical, strange voices rang out. She was pleasantly surprised by this unexpected success, and accepted Bugsy's invitation to lay her head on his stretched out body. The strange, yet amusing voices crackled on and all her guests seemed relaxed and happy.

'How did you get your nickname, Bugsy?' asked June as she turned her head to get a closer look at his handsome face. She was fascinated that one so young was already a potential blue beard and was having to shave already.

'My *broer* is a [iv]tug hand.' He answered. 'So that's where I get the name'. He concluded.

June could not quite see the logic in it. 'What does the name Tug have to do with Bugsy?

'Well Tug rhymes with Bug, but I didn't like Bug so I changed it to Bugsy.' He answered with conviction.

shouldn't that be your brother's name then?' she asked.

'No his name is Francois.'

June thought about it for a moment, it didn't make sense, but then, lately, nothing seemed to make sense to her, especially at certain times of the month. Her eyes became heavy and she realized she needed to get some sleep on her tobacco filled bed, as the next day was the beginning of term again.

CHAPTER 6

'If the sun refuse to shine,
I'll still be loving you
When mountains crumble to the sea,
there will still be you and me.'
Led Zeppelin 1968

'I'm sorry, Pleeze let me go' came the pleading cries from the football grounds. Steven was fifteen and had presented himself as an argumentative lad seeking attention from the others. He was tolerated, because most of the time, he was simply ignored. But now, he was on the brink of tears, as a bigger and stronger youth, two years his senior, was sitting on top of him, torturously, twisting his arm back.

'are you sure your sorry?' taunted the older boy 'say pretty please'.

'Pretty please' stammered the younger one 'Pleeze I'm sorry.' He was genuinely in distress. Still, the older lad with blonde hair flopping around his face, would not accept his anguished pleas. His perfectly chiselled profile could be seen starkly against the shadows of the oncoming twilight. June and the others looked on in awe at the sight of their friend getting the beating of his life by this new boy on the block.

'I guess he's marking his new territory......well Steve had it coming to him' commented Shawn, who was already secretly deciding to keep well away from this older and stronger boy, named Murray. He shrugged his shoulders and walked away. The game of slow motion football which had kept the girls in fits of laughter had come to an abrupt end, and now all eyes were diverted to this young blonde fighter, who sat astride his vanquished foe. Over the months June had acquired a bit more cleavage. It had slightly shaped the rest of her boyish body. Her chest heaved anxiously. She was acquainted with the likes of bullies and the scene before her made her feel apprehensive. She was not impressed, yet secretly she was curious to get to know the victor better.

The sun had gone down rather quickly and soon the football field was in darkness, but she could still see his blonde hair blowing in the breeze. At last he released the troubled victim and ambled over to where the girls were still standing. His eyes immediately fell upon June, and her heart began to beat faster. She had experienced having a boyfriend or two but the relationship had never lasted long. In fact the boys had defined her as quite a 'frigid chick'. Perhaps this was because of the impressions she had as a twelve year old, who had time to ponder the plight of her sister.

Mandy and Tom had given her enough visual education in the field of sex. Every weekend on the couch the drama unfolded. As they lay together, pretending to be asleep. Tom's hand like a ship following a strong current often harboured in an 'out of bounds' area on Mandy's curvy body only to be turned away promptly, when he tried to 'dock' and so the struggle would ensue....constantly, as the battle for

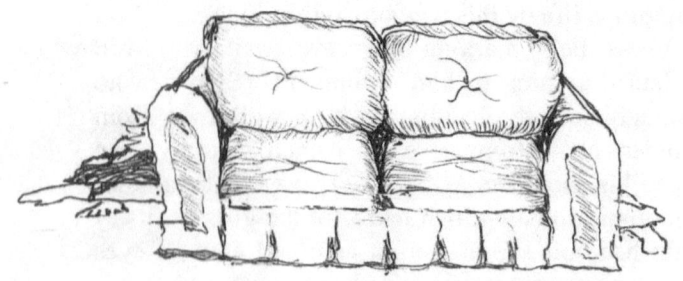

territory continued. Inevitably the romp on the couch gravitated to the surrender behind the couch, followed by the recovery of two very dishevelled looking lovers. This had left June muddled about all things sexual, and such a muddle was contagious to her potential boyfriends, who found her mixed signals too confusing. For, as she fumbled around in her conscience trying to sort out a code which would set clear boundaries, the boy had, in the meantime, lost interest and was moving on to someone whose morality was a little more simple. To win this lad over she would have to sort herself out quickly, she decided.

***

June's face was tear stained, she had been crying incessantly. The frustration was apparent, by the way she perched herself at the top of the stairs, while Murray stood in a more subservient position below her. It had become a regular place to iron out their differences and had always ended up with them collapsed in each other's arms in tears. They assumed that no-one could hear them but it was clear by the unusual silence, and the lack of people coming in and out of their flats, that the whole of the 11th floor was enjoying the 'soap'. What they lacked in entertainment due to the fact that television had still not been introduced into the country, they made up with a reality show on their doorsteps.

'I just want to be free' she wailed. 'Murray, let me go, I can't do this anymore!' She was pleading with him now. She sobbed pathetically.

It had been 10 months since they had met and the relationship had developed rapidly from a flirtatious and experimental encounter to a harrowing and all too serious attachment. All her other friends had vanished over the months and she felt alienated and consumed by Murray's all pervading presence.

'But I love you Junie, I want you more than anything in the world...just admit it... that's what you want too...to be mine.. in every way.... physically...I mean..as well as every other way..' he replied dramatically.

Murray was half Irish and half Italian and this combination of backgrounds caused him to be not only an extreme romantic but also very definite about what he wanted at that moment in time...June's body.

'I'm only 14!' She screeched in frustration. 'can't you cool it! I want to at least finish school'

'But why, when you've got me?' His deep voice reverberated down the corridor.

'Got you?...You don't even go to work! You fantasize about work, but everyone's seen you sitting in the park all day, feeding the pigeons.'

'Who! Tell me and I'll knock their block off'

'Ohhh Murray that's not the point!!'

He came towards her to try and make up as usual and she pushed him away, back down the stairs.

'All right, I give up' she cried, 'take me, take all of meeee....' she flung herself across the stair railings, and hurt herself as she did it, which made her cry more. Murray began to cry. He wondered why this girl hadn't fallen for him 'hook, line and sinker' like the others had. After all it was 1969, and everyone was making love. He could have anyone he wanted. But he wanted 'Miss June' and until he possessed her completely he would not be happy, nevertheless, ravishing her in the state that she was in, being as distressed as she clearly was, even to his mind was unfair. 'Listen Junie, Listen to me. I'll go away, I'll go to Jeffries bay for awhile... give you time to think about things.'

At these words, June stopped crying immediately. She glared at him, and wiped the tears away, and blew her nose on her bell sleeve.

'You will, you really will? She stammered, her voice quavering like that of an old lady.

'yes, I'll go away for awhile...surfing...Jeffries'

'but you don't even like surfing, you only like fighting.' She was suddenly suspicious, but decided to leave it at that, just in case he changed his mind.

Silence pervaded for a moment and he clambered up to her and put his arm around her. She plopped her tired head down on his shoulder, and sniffled. At that moment windows began to open and radios went on and Ken's front door creaked open as he casually trotted down the stairs, glimpsing back at June's swollen tear stained face.

For a young girl of fourteen, ten months in a possessive relationship had been far too long. She felt she had already forgotten what it was to have friends. The little juvenile was still such a novice at the art of socializing and it had been prematurely terminated, but the taste of freedom made her realize that she could not go back to that stifling relationship again, and why should she? Life was to be enjoyed.

So, a period of peace followed and she felt intoxicated with her new freedom. To frolic in the water with her girl friends and tease the boys playfully, was the height of happiness to her. Oh how great it was to be free from the restrictions that came with having a steady boyfriend.

Unfortunately, the wonderfully indulgent feeling of liberty, came to an abrupt end when Murray returned. He found her down at the beach and his fury knew no limits... Beach, boys, and little Ken, was all he could see around his girlfriend. With long calculated strides, he made his way to the girl with the long brown hair whose suntanned, freckly shoulders were powdered with salt from the sea. The humiliated lad looked down on her carefree, smiling face and spoke to her heatedly under his breath.

"I want to talk to you." He demanded gruffly. Her smile disappeared, and only a slight frown expressed her true feelings to her carefree companions that there was tension in the air. Clambering to her feet, she commenced to saunter reluctantly by his side until they got to the road leading home.

"Come on, you are going home right now" He demanded as he grabbed her by the arm.

"Oh no, I'm not! You can't tell me what to do, who do you think you are? You don't own me!" she shouted, surprised at her new found courage. At this he grabbed her by the hair and dragged her down the street towards her home.

"I won't go! I won't go!" she screamed. With a fistful of her hair he continued to pull her along, while she hurled abuse at him. The screaming continued until they reached the corner of the street. It was not surprising that by the time the performance was done, the onlookers were laughing from their balconies and enjoying the entertainment that they were so deprived of.

Eventually in desperation she tore herself loose and ran all the way up eleven flights of stairs into the safe presence of her dad who was sitting, as usual , reading his newspaper, seemingly unaware of the enfolding drama that had been played out over the last ten months.

"What on earth is wrong?" he asked as he flipped the corner of the newspaper back to look at his bedraggled daughter. In her distress she burst into long heart rendering sobs.

Its him" she cried "He's horrible,... I hate him,..... I never want to see him again. He..He.. hurt me!" she was crying so much that she had to take big gasps of breath between every word.

This was all too much for her Dad, who unexpectedly took control of the situation. It was as if he had been anticipating such a moment for a long time. Slowly and deliberately he rose to his feet and calmly went to the kitchen where mother stood with her dish cloth, anxiously drying her hands.

"I won't be long" he said to her in a calculating manner

"I'm just going to buy some milk". He picked up an empty glass milk bottle and went out the door, gently closing it behind him.

Timidly, the tear stained teen peaked over the balcony only to see the older man conversing with the well built lad.. Only once did she see the foreboding figure of her dad, wave the milk bottle in his face. At that, Murray, turned on his heels and disappeared down the street.

June had learnt an important lesson and she promised herself that she would not get locked into another unhealthy relationship. She cringed inside, as she thought of what could have happened, had she carried through her words to give herself completely to him. The experience had left her wiser but also harder at heart. Something that comes with age. It was a warning sign that she was growing up much too fast and needed to slow down. Would it be possible to slow down? Yes,.. it was imperative for her well being that she pace herself...before she got into trouble. How this was to be done was a mystery to her.

CHAPTER 7

'Let it Be' Beatles 1968

June turned to look at her friend who slept beside her. She rubbed her eyes which were stiff with Mascara, and opened the curtains. Everything from the night before came flooding back into her mind. Murray had seized her on the dance floor, and had forced her to dance. He had held her so tightly that she could hardly breathe. The tussle that followed with the other boys, when they worked out what was going on, had given them an excuse to whip up a fight. Once more, Murray was in the middle of it all. In fear, June had run away as fast as she could and ended up in someone's back garden, pinned against the fence with an enormous dog barking at her. What an upsetting night it had been.

Her friend, Irene, looked so peaceful lying there with her strawberry blond hair flayed across the pillow, but June knew that she had her own problems too deal with. The image of her fun loving friend, gazing in awe at the Asian drummer on the stage was not easy to dismiss. Irene was love struck for a boy who was, in the South African context, the wrong colour. But Irene did not worry about such things. She was adamant that Jackie, the lean, young Asian man, with the beautiful smile was meant for her. It did not matter what the world thought about it.

June quickly diverted her stare away from her, as Irene stretched, then yawned and opened her almond shaped eyes towards the window. Only a patch of blue sky could be seen, as the bright sun peaked around the corner of one of the city blocks and shed its brightness directly into Irene's green eyes. She winced and moved her head into the shade of the waving curtain.

'Close the curtain a bit June.' She ordered. June submitted. She was a few years younger than the tall red head, and was a little puzzled, yet flattered in a way that Irene would want to associate with the likes of her. They lay there deep in thought, silently recalling the previous night's developments. The sound of the sea could be heard in the distance, and a pigeon cooed on a balcony close by.

'You know, June, Murray really loves you.' Said Irene, her voice still rough from sleep. 'you should be glad of such love'. She continued.

'He's just a possessive fool' came the reply. June turned over to light her first cigarette of the day.

'You're so ruthless!' mumbled Irene. June, dangled her legs over the side of the bed and inhaled deeply on her cigarette. She thought for a moment, and could not conceive that she was ruthless. She was just thoroughly tired of the whole drama and longed to move on in her life. There was so much to see and do, why should she be stuck in this same old groove like a record hooked on a line of a song, over and over again, saying ' June's doomed to a life with Murray'. Anyway what a boring subject it was. She turned her attention to a much more interesting thought. Cautiously, launching into the subject of the dark, handsome drummer, she asked,

'So...what's the drummer's name then?' she could not hide her curiosity.

'You know very well what his name is.' retorted Irene, pushing back the bed covers with great energy.

'why do you want to know anyway?'

'Well I think he really digs you, he couldn't take his eyes off you' June answered in a condescending way, a little regretful that she had approached the subject in the first place, and not sure where it was all going. It was evident that June had stepped over the line, by invading Irene's privacy. After all she was definitely not qualified to be the older girl's confidante.

'I'm going to see Jackie today, you wanna come with?' Irene inquired briskly, as she padded into the bathroom. June nodded weakly. She had not expected to be invited to accompany her friend to see the young drummer.

It was time for her to get dressed then, so she slid out of bed and looked in the full length mirror. Compared to Irene, her body was shapeless. She began to strap her bikini top on. It was clear that her reflection did not please her. Posing in front of the mirror, she tried to imagine a body worthy of a bikini with no tee shirt to hide the flaws.

'We're meeting Lesley in town' continued Irene, as she plodded back into the bedroom, toothbrush in hand. She stopped abruptly, to take note of June's pose in front of the mirror,

'What are you doing now, you little poser!' she exclaimed,

'You know what, it's not that you're ruthless, it's just that you only love one person and *that's* yourself!' The words tumbled out of her mouth as if they had been well rehearsed.

June sank onto the bed, she felt embarrassed and out of her depth, and did not know what to say. It was no use telling the older girl about how she really felt about herself, it would just sound pretentious and she felt so shallow as it was. To forgive her friend for her lack of insight was the only way to go.

Mother had given June enough money to buy some material from the oriental bazaar. She discovered that she had a flare for fashion and enjoyed sewing, finding it quite therapeutic. Being sent shopping for fabric, was a convenient excuse to go with Irene to meet Jackie.

Saturday morning was hot and busy, the town was crowded. A statue of Queen Victoria stood erect and proud in the town square. June often forgot that she was in Africa. It was oh so, British, not a black person could be seen anywhere, only the signboards saying 'no blacks allowed' reminded her of the sinister, yet fragile disposition that her and all her kin held.

Blissfully distracted by other things, the three girls made their way into the heart of another world which lay on the peripheries of the centre of town. This was the world of the 'non-whites'. Here, there were no big department stores with special lighting and expensive western goods, where everything appeared ordered and respectable. This was the world where all the senses came alive. It was a fiasco of colour, as the beautiful silks and cottons, were neighbour to the stalls donning ointments and spices, giving off pungent sweet smells which permeated the air all about. The sound of bartering and excitement was all around, as fruit and vegetables were changing hands. Mothers chatted loudly from the nearby tenement flats as they went about hanging their washing from the windows. In the disarray and turmoil of the moment there was an unexplainable charm that June could not quite grasp.

She followed the two girls silently, feeling shy and out of her depth. There was a sense that everyone was looking at them and well could they have been, seeing that the three young girls were the only white people around.

'So where does he live?' she heard Irene say to a lad who appeared out of a dark lane. His starched, white shirt looked slick against his polished, amber skin. He pointed to a rundown tenement building, describing which floor and door to go to.

While they continued to chat, June found herself standing on the threshold of a squalid little shop. She peered into the darkness and noticed an elderly African man squatting on a low stool. He gave her a toothless smile and beckoned her inside. She felt compelled to comply and smiled back at him. [v] He began to show her his wares.   Knarled, rotten carcasses of dead animals were hanging precariously from hooks. All sorts of curious body organs floated in the waters of grubby bottles. Snake skins draped from the ceiling, moved in the slightness of a mysterious breeze which seemed to come from nowhere. He waved his bony finger around the shop, proudly and gestured to her that she could have anything she liked if she crossed his palms with cash. June motioned with her hand that she didn't need any potions, be it for love or revenge, and she backed out of the shop, her face frozen in the same smile that she entered with.

She looked around and found that the girls were moving off without her and hastened to catch up with them.

It did not take long to find Jackie within the dark corridors of his tenement building. He looked around suspiciously and seemed not as delighted to see Irene as she was to see him.

'Did anyone see you come here?' he asked nervously. She shook her head and feretted her way into his arms forcing a cuddle out of him. The contented red head seemed satisfied with the warmth she had succeeded in generating from him, even if it was engineered more from her side but the magic moment was abruptly broken by Lesley's interjection.

'You know I've come to score. I hope you have the grass'.

'Not today' answered Jackie bluntly.

Why not, how could you let me down?' came the impatient reply.

'Because the feds are sure to follow three white girls through Indian town... you should know that.' He answered quickly, making an effort to restrain his irritation.

Lesley tutted. And swore under her breath 'Come on June, lets leave Irene to it. There's nothing here for us.'

She took June by her tie dyed teeshirt and dragged her out into the sunlight, leaving Irene's weak protests to fade into the distance. The angry, robust girl who presented herself as quite masculine, stalked speedily back to the centre of town with June close at her heels.

'I don't know where this relationship is leading, I guess it will end in a pile of shite. She'll be back, she'll come back to me that's for sure.' She muttered under her breath.

CHAPTER 8

*'Good, Good, Good, Good vibrations. Beach Boys
1966*

June had closed her curtains against the noonday sun.
She welcomed the semi darkness and the coolness that
it produced. It seemed to reflect the thoughts that were
going on in her head. She couldn't quite put her finger
on what was wrong, and why she felt, at times, so
inadequate and not up to standard in so many ways.

'I'm fairly good looking' she reasoned, and then in
alarm, rebuked herself. 'how shallow I am! looks
aren't everything, its my personality....its flawed. I
need to be more fun to have fun' came the next erratic
thought. A feeling of self disdain crept up on her. It
was evident that the sporadic spells of fun were already
becoming an end in themselves.

She nestled her head deeper into the pillow hoping
that the downy softness, would comfort her enough to
confirm that she wasn't such a bad person after all.

An optimistic outlook, was not within grasp, at that
particular moment in time and suddenly she was able to
understand why she was feeling so down. Mandy's
voice became more distinct from the lounge. This was
their last day in Durban, as they had decided to start
afresh and make a go of their failing marriage by
returning to Tom's home town in Rhodesia.

It had been five years since Tom had been put on a
train, by his mother, at the tender age of sixteen, with
only a duffle bag and a packed lunch. Arriving in
Durban with nowhere to go, and no one to look after
him, he was forced to make a living for himself and

41

learn't how to survive on his own. It was very hard for him, but he made good.

Now they were leaving, leaving a big hole in June's heart, she could only wish them the best, but suddenly she felt so alone. It was not possible for her to cheerfully say goodbye, it was better that she lay in the semi darkness of her room and waited for them to go.

Suddenly the door opened and big sister stepped to the side of her bed where she was laying. The fragrance of her perfume spread through the room. She always smelt so nice. June had spent many a morning watching Mandy dressing. Oh what a ritual it was! First the deodorant, then the powder, then the stockings, the perfume, and the actual dressing and then to end it all, the copious amount of hairspray to keep the teased up hair intact. So much hairspray that June would stumble to the window throwing it open, to take great gasps of air.

It seemed odd, that June was going to miss her sister so much especially since they crossed swords on more than one occasion, but she had to admit that she would feel lost without her sister and *that*, she decided, was the source of her gloominess.

Mandy stooped down and gathered June up in her arms. The tenderness surprised the younger sister, and she felt overwhelmed with emotion.

'Listen little sister, I forgive you for all those times that you stole my clothes and wore them without asking me first, I love you, and I will keep in touch.' June's eyes welled up with tears, and for a moment sibling rivalry was diffused, as they looked into each other's tear filled eyes. Tommy appeared from behind, he hesitated for a moment and then said, 'come on, Mandy, we'll be late for the train.' Then it was his turn to scoop June up in his arms and give her a big kiss and then they were gone.

She hoped that they would be safe, even though there were already rumours of sanctions been set up in the country and [vi]war was imminent on the borders of Rhodesia. Hopefully they would return if there was turmult in the country.

***

It was September, the time of the rainy season, and the Michaelmas holidays had begun. Irrespective of this, June found herself sitting at the dining room table trying to concentrate on her homework. She was getting increasingly worried about her exams which were not far away. The familiar sound of the radio droned on in the background, and helped her to concentrate.

1969 had arrived, but television had not. A visually deprived, and information hungry South Africa, could only partially partake of the important world events that had been unfolding. Much was censored from South African ears through the suppression of BBC. [vii]Nelson Mandela was in prison on Robin Island, and June could not understand why he was such a threat to the government. She could hear his name mentioned again over the news as usual and she stopped what she was doing to listen for a moment. It was as if the present regime was reassuring the country that all was well. Nelson Mandela was still stuck away in a cell and would most probably die there.

She chewed on her pen for a moment and thought about her dad's words.

[viii]'As long as the Dutch man is in power we have nothing to worry about,' he would say, sitting in his armchair looking very comfortable.

She knew that South Africa was mighty unpopular and excluded from the rest of the world. Not even the news could hide that fact. The Apartheid laws had cut the country off from everything. She felt mildly disturbed, but shrugged it off

'Oh well', she thought, 'as long as I can get my music from abroad, I'm happy' she concluded and went back to her maths equation, but another thorn in the government's flesh was mentioned and once more her ears pricked up, this time it was the [ix]South African Council of Churches.

'These churches are causing such trouble in the country' piped up mother from the kitchen. June strained her ears to hear what they had been up to now, but the news was muffled by her mother's loud ramblings. 'How can churches be so involved in politics... aren't they only supposed to address spiritual things? Either that or the Vicars should just go into politics and stop hiding behind the cloth.'

for special effects she threw the plates into the sink and a loud dramatic clang followed.

June sighed deeply, and closed her books, resigning herself to the fact that she was not going to get any work done there where feelings were running high.

She went to her room, and gazed out the window at the rain. It was set in for the holidays, that she knew. What the plans were for the holidays, she could only guess. The surf was sure to be good as it was the time for the spring tides, but on the other hand an undiscerning surfer could find himself in a tricky situation in those very big waves, if he wasn't careful. She thought of one of the girl surfer's, Ellen. Oh Ellen was so beautiful!. The way she emerged from the waves, surf board in hand and her overflowing bikini top hoisted up by string. How she kept it together only added to the mystery around this beautiful athletic girl. She had no inhibitions.

'When I'm a few years older, I intend to be like Ellen', thought June. 'A goddess in everyway, with all the cool dudes feeding out of my hand.' She caught her thoughts again and was astonished at her desire for popularity.

At that moment the proverbial 'saved by the bell' happened as the phone rang and June grasped the receiver with relief...someone was saving her from her thoughts, she could only be grateful for that.

'Hi June we're at Bugsy's today, come over?' Annie's friendly voice reverberated down the receiver and invoked an immediate response from June. She scrambled into her Levi jeans and strapped on her leather sandals and wasted no more time as she skipped right over to Bugsy's place.

His Mum and Dad had gone away for a few days, and Bugsy found himself home alone, except for the occasional appearance of his big brother.

The door opened slowly to the sight of a dark room and the kids sat around on the floor looking very solemn. She broke the silence by greeting her circle of friends cheerfully but was met by expressionless faces which, momentarily directed their attention at her and then returned to the task at hand. She peered into the middle of the circle and wondered what all the fuss was about. Why everyone was focused so intently on a mirror placed on the floor with a glass on it, briefly puzzled her. Until with a whisper, Bugsy explained that they were waiting for the spirits to come, so they needed to be very quiet and concentrate until the mission was accomplished.

June felt tense, but placed herself quietly down beside her handsome friend.

At the Christian camp, in her half interested state she vaguely remembered being warned against such activities, but hey, was it not a viable excuse to get close to this lad who she liked? At that present moment, there was nothing she would rather do than sit in a dark place with Bugsy, they might even steal a kiss or two in the process she fancied.

The phenomenon of young people able to concentrate and focus, even for an hour would have caused a school master's heart to warm towards his students, but to focus for hours on end was incomprehensible! Only the jangling sound of the girls' wrist bangles could be heard as they removed their tired fingers, now and again, from the glass. The minutes turned into hours and as the mugs of tea and smokes were passed around, there was also the laborious occupation of staying awake and keeping vigilant.

The next day saw the same ritual, and then on the third day, as the heavy glass stood forlornly in the middle of the circle surrounded by the dancing reflections bouncing off the mirror, there was a stir and then another. A sound of grinding was detected, as the glass took on a life of its own and began to move slowly around the mirror, like a spinning top in slow motion. It spun in such a way that all suspicions of it being a figment of the imagination disappeared and was replaced, instead by astonishment , as each awestruck observer gazed at the spectacle before them. Suddenly the ominous activity was no longer entertaining and an eerie sensation culminated in a cold tingle down June's spine. Showing signs of panic, Jeannie checked to see that no-one was pushing the glass, as all fingers were still lightly placed on the top of the crystal object.

'Where do we go from here?' whispered Annie. Bugsy shrugged his shoulders and shiftily looked from face to face. Shadows danced on each disturbed countenance and as if mesmerised, they kept their eyes focused on the spectacle. The seconds turned to

46

minutes, then June eventually cleared her throat and broke the silence. She was reluctant to remain at her post, to see what message the spirit or spirits would transmit. It was enough to know that they were present. Had not the mission been accomplished? Now was the time to split, she decided.

'I think I'm going to make tracks home' her voice was croaky from lack of use. Much to her surprise, Mouse, Steve and Mark followed suit.

The foursome stumbled into the fresh air that smelt of rain. June rubbed her eyes. She had been sitting in the darkness for so long and found herself having trouble adapting to the sudden brightness of the white light. The pavements were looking clean and glittery, even pure. The girl felt like running and playing in them, but as they were all feeling hungry they ventured to the corner store instead. Christos the Greek store keeper stood behind the counter, as usual. He was a comforting sight, even though at times his patience was painfully tried by the clamour of too many teenagers scrambling for cool drinks and snacks all at once. It was hard for him to keep tabs of so many of them but at this particular moment, he stood tranquilly behind the counter relishing a moment of quietness before the next wave of customers rolled over the threshold into his small, overloaded shop.

'Do you think it's possible,' began Steve as he leant over the counter and peered intensely into the store keeper's face

'for a heavy glass to twirl around, on the floor, unaided, I mean it was spinning man....of course we had our fingers on it... very lightly...but still'.

The store keeper, who was still in a pensive frame of mind thought for a second or two, then, with the air of a scientist, sought to put the troubled enquirer's mind at ease by answering, 'yes I guess so... mmmm...perhaps the heat from all your grubby little fingers caused it to move...heat can cause movement...can it not?' he replied in his stilted accent 'but I don't know about the spinning?' he added, as an afterthought.

'Thanks, bye' came the reply. Steve sprang away from the counter collected up his goods, and beckoned the others to follow. Nothing more was said of the bizarre episode. It couldn't be explained, so it was better to forget it ever happened.

CHAPTER 9

'Chasing shadows over my walls' Deep Purple 1969

As the holidays went on the weather didn't improve and indoor activities became harder to conjure up. There was a mutual agreement amongst the little band that the spirits were better left alone as the activity had become too eerie, even for the resolute ones, like Jeannie and Bugsy.

Totally by chance, the next adventure that the inquisitive friends stumbled upon was at the other end of the spectrum from the previous activity. Being the observant one in the group, Annie directed everyone's attention to a series of posters carefully displayed around the area.

'Come to *LifeBeat* coffee bar, music, refreshments and fun, all welcome at Christ Church, Addington.' It read.

'Cool, a coffee bar, tonight lets go!' announced Steve enthusiastically.

'wait...its at a church' interjected Ken, as he pushed his way to the front to get a closer look at the small print.

'Oh bumma...maybe not then' resounded a voice in the midst of the group.

'Nah, lets go anyway, what else is there to do. At least its free' declared Bugsy. At the mention of the magic word *free,* all answered with one accord, 'Ok lets go!'

So, that night, the parish church burst at the seams with the local beach crowd, who expected to be well entertained . Woe to the organisers if this could not be delivered, the expressions of which, turned from pleasant surprise to flurried apprehension as more and more scantily clad young ruffians, who were blissfully unaware of the boundaries in such an environment, filed past them. The flustered Christian visionaries could, at that present moment only visualize a volatile situation that could possibly accelerate out of control.

As expected, the night became quite rowdy until the youth leader who was a Cliff Richard look-a-like with a Beatle's haircut, got up on the stage and introduced himself as Simon. No-one seemed too interested in what he had to say until he handed over to a young girl on a guitar who immediately launched into song. The lyrics were new to June. She tried to match them up with the angry, brusque lyrics which she had intentionally acquired a taste for. At first she thought how sentimental and lame the whole scene was, but soon became captured by the words that were being sung.

'supersonic jets are flying,
space ships speed across the sky.
Down below a man is dying but no-one hears his cry.
No-one hears, no-one hears in the sadness
in the darkness, no-one hears.'

The lyrics touched a chord in the curious girl's heart. Who was the song about? Was it perhaps suffering humanity or Jesus? She wondered.
'See the Son of Man dying on a cross...'
'Oh it's Jesus'...question answered.' She deduced, taking note of the fact that the girl was a senior from her school, and toying with the idea of marking and avoiding her when she saw her again in the corridors.

Suddenly she felt a tug on her suade jacket. It was Lucy.

'Hey, Luke's at *Wind and Sea*, Hey June please come with me. I need to see him.' June gazed at Lucy with concern in her eyes. She had been looking quite wretched the past few months. She peered back at the stage for a moment. It was no use, it was time to go. Lucy was so needy and so love sick, of course she would go with her to the night club.

Wind and Sea was one of those night clubs, known by the initiated few. It was tucked away in a dark alley somewhere in the back streets of Durban. June had only heard about the place, but had never had the opportunity to go there. But tonight was her chance, seeing that her mum thought she was at a Christian coffee Bar and she still had a few hours to spare. It did not take much badgering from Lucy to persuade her to go. As the soloist continued to sing her heart out to the revellers who were not sure what to make of the gig, they turned on their heels and out the door they ran.

'Hey June its so nice to see you' called a voice from behind her, as they were fleeing. A young woman with long black hair, her smiling husband in tow, came sauntering up to her. June recognized them as neighbours who lived in her building. They were a friendly but stubborn couple, stubborn because they did not seem to know when to stop harassing the disinterested family, by incessantly inviting them to church. Nevertheless, they displayed great joy at seeing June attending the Coffee bar.

'Not now!' thought June as she forced a smile on her face. She responded appropriately, but made it clear that she was in a hurry to get away. Lucy continued to pull her along. She scuttled along in reverse away from the couple, and all she could do was wave at them. Once more they turned on their heels and disappeared around the corner.

Down the dark streets they sprinted, their long hair flowing behind them. The rain had stopped at last and in its place, the air felt salty and moist on their skin. Lucy's passion for Luke, presented June with an opportune reason to satisfy her curiosity and seek out the club which was whispered about among an emerging alternate minority.

At last they entered a dark, narrow alley. It was so dark that they could hardly see one foot in front of them. They followed the sound of underground music and the faint glimmer of light at the end of the road. As the music got louder, so the light became brighter and a pungent smell of smoke, wafted in the air. Faces appeared out of the shadows, faces that June did not recognise, alluring and exciting. Young men, clean shaven with crew cuts, leaned against the brick walls, many of them had green trench coats on, which could only mean that they were doing their time in the army. Others wore their hair long, and were proud of their downy looks. This group of lads had, in some crafty way beaten the system and had avoided the compulsory call up into the army. Beach babes donned the pavements, having disposed of their raincoats. Even though they shivered in the cold, they seized the opportunity to show off their beautiful bodies and their colourful crop tops and hipsters displayed their taut, tanned waists and ample bosoms.

In the half light of a lamp, June recognized her friend Irene, sitting on the wet pavement. She was cradling her head in the cleft of another girl's shoulder. It was Lesley. Holding Irene close, she comforted and caressed her lovingly. June strolled towards them and knelt down to greet them. Irene looked wasted and miserable. Before June could say anything, Irene blurted out.

'He's dead, he died in a motor accident.' June knew right away that she was talking about her Asian boyfriend, Jackie. She lean't forward to comfort her, but was warded off by Lesley who felt she was the only one who had the right to touch her. Recovering herself, June moved away, but coaxed her with gentle words of condolences. Lesley looked at her harshly and continued to stroke Irene affectionately.

At that moment Lucy yanked at June's jacket sleeve and steered her towards the entrance of the club.

Hawkwind was playing on the floor above them and a rickety spiral stair case saw them to their destination.

Inside the cavern of darkness. white lights flashed, revealing one solitary dancer on the dance floor, who moved like Charlie Chaplin in an old silent, silver screen movie. Except it wasn't silent... the lyrics were bellowing out

'Where freedom reigns on minds of peace.
Minds rich in wisdom to the last.
We are children of the sun
and this is our inheritance.'

June wondered why no-one was dancing, she was used to clubs where boys asked girls to dance with them to docile songs like John Lennon's 'Let it be', but this club was different. Everyone was absorbed in their own world, only a single soul twirled and dipped with his arms outstretched around the dance floor. His tassled jacket hanging carelessly off his shoulders.
'Who is that cat?' shouted June in Lucy's ear. The lights flashed white again. Lucy's pale lips read
'Luke'.

June took a second look at the lad zooming around the room imitating a fighter jet. So it was! This is where he had been hiding all these months, it was obvious that he had freed himself from all his inhibitions.

'He looked so different.... a bit like the vocalist from the [x]"Who", with his platinum blonde hair hanging all over his face'. thought June.

She could not, somehow, imagine him going back to a life of sports and academics, but then she remembered him saying to his friends that there was no use being competitive in the sports world because [xi]South Africa was banned from the Olympics anyway. He had a point, she supposed.

All those things that had been rumoured about him were true then. He was flying high. High on LSD, consumed in a world of surrealism. Perhaps in the not far future, he would come back to reality, but at that present moment, it seemed pretty doubtful.

June did not dare to look at Lucy, but instinctively felt her pain. She had surely lost him to something more ominous than another girl.

The daily local newspaper had been strategically placed on the table on the page that read in bold letters: **Addington boy attempts to swim to Australia**. June's eyes could not help but see the article. Her mother's timely entrance into the room and June's alarmed expression, only confirmed the watchful woman's suspicions, yet nothing was said.

Yes, Luke had finally snapped. His many trips on LSD was taking its toll upon his mind. He was now locked up in a psychiatric hospital. When he was to be released was anyone's guess.

'What a goof ball!', muttered June, hoping that her air of indifference would put her mother off the scent, steering her away from the fact that the night it happened was quite traumatic to say the least. For, after leaving the club with Lucy and Luke and his big brother, Seth, Luke had lost control and sprinted down to the water's edge. He was a strong swimmer but this did not change the inevitable and he was soon floundering in deep, dark waters. All the shouting and struggling that ensued between him and his brother out in the stormy waves, could not sway him from his mission. In his befuddled state... he was off to Australia.

The images of police, ambulances, sirens, lifesavers, ropes and oxygen, were still vivid in June's mind.

To share these things with her mother was the furthest thing from her mind. She really didn't need to be burdened with maternal tensions. She would like to have unburdened herself with the news of Irene's boyfriend's death, but she felt, even that was a little too controversial a subject for her mother to handle, because he was the wrong skin colour.

Smiling nonchalantly she glided through the room and headed towards the fridge. But the silence only strengthened her mother's gnawing suspicions. She had a gut feeling that June was hiding something. The article had failed to evoke any lasting reaction, but that did not shift her from her goal... to get information out of her daughter.

June began to hum as she rummaged in the fridge looking for a snack

The determined woman cleared her throat, as she prepared to torment June with a torrent of questions.

'Isn't Luke that lovely lad who plays foot ball so well?

There was a moment of silence, as June tried to think of something to say which would change the subject.

Suddenly the phone rang, June closed the fridge. She had lost her appetite anyway.

'Mandy, darling, oh so wonderful to hear your voice how are you, how is Tommy, has he joined the army yet?' Mother stumbled over her words excitedly.

At last she had the satisfaction of questions being answered, even if it was from another source.

June returned to her room, quickly. She had successfully squirmed out of *that* confrontation thanks to her sister's timeliness.

'He has, Oh dear, I hope he'll be alright, and you are you doing ok?' She heard her mother say, then, there was a long pause.

'Alright darling, well whatever you need....light bulbs.....yes love, I'll send them to you.....what do the Brits think their doing! Sanctions!.....ridiculous, totally ridiculous!'

June heard the click of the receiver.

There was a knock at the door. Samson the flat boy entered, he had a white spotless uniform on. June could hear her mother giving him instructions. He was to start cleaning in *her* room. The floors needed polishing.

'We're coming in!' warned mother as the door swung opened and the two people spilled into her bedroom. June sat swinging on her chair in front of her dressing table, she was all legs, just a tee shirt over her knickers. She sat and looked as her mother took a deep breath and launched into a conversation, June braced herself.

'Do you know what Tommy's friend, Harry, has to do in the army?'

June exhaled and responded a little too eagerly, as she moved her legs out of the way so that Samson could polish under her chair.

'No what?'

'He has to prove how many terrorists he has killed by cutting off an ear from each of his victims and presenting them to the authorities.'

'Wow' came the answer.

Samson continued to clean around the bed. His black skin was wet with sweat and he smelt bad. The smell was distracting.

'Samson you can start on the windows now please' Mother gave him a sweet smile. He clambered up onto his feet, his knees were gnarled from kneeling. Quietly he set about preparing to climb out of the window and clean.

'Well, I hope that Tom won't have to do such a shitty task' answered June.

'He better not be doing such a terrible thing.....I think Harry is a mercenary or something...and by the way, don't swear.'

'Hmm' June looked pensively at Samson as he hung precariously out of the window, doing his best to clean the outermost corners of the panes.

She felt a bit uncomfortable.

'Ok Mum you can go now and take Samson with you please.'

With bucket in hand Samson was summoned out of the room and the door shut behind them.

'Peace at last' thought June as she fiddled with her make-up.

'This mascara is the best! It makes my eyelashes look so long.' She said to herself.

CHAPTER 10

'Plastic people,
Oh Baby, now,
You're such a drag.'
Frank Zappa 1966

June discovered that little Ken had a sister. She first saw them on the street, deep in conversation. A heavy kit bag was slung over the girl's shoulder. Her long, dark hair was piled on top of her head, skillfully held there by a chop stick. It turned out that she had run away from home to be with her boyfriend who was living in an outhouse on top of a garage just a few yards away from Ken's own home. Ken's dad had no idea that his daughter, Isabelle, had hitch hiked all the way from Cape Town and was in Durban. She had insisted that Ken not tell him. It was a convenient coincidence that June meandered past them that afternoon and the encounter ended in June storing Isabelle's kit bag in her room while the run away girl went to sort out her affairs with her boyfriend.

Her boyfriend was a handsome young man with dark hair and piercing brown eyes. He boasted of having stowed away to Australia, and also of escaping from prison more than once, hence he was known for his great escapes and admired accordingly.

After a day or two, Isabelle politely collected her few possessions from June's flat and moved into the out house with her boyfriend.

The arrangement went well for awhile, until the novelty wore off. It only took a few weeks for him to grow disinterested in her.

From June's bedroom window the saga unfolded. Isabelle, sitting, forlornly outside his place. Occasionally, June could see her knocking on his door. Sometimes June would gravitate towards the window and look out of it, wondering if Isabelle had gained entrance. She was successful at times, but there were other times that she wasn't. In spite of all this, the slip of a girl would not let her dad know that she was only a 'stone's throw' away from him.

Much to June's relief, the routine faded out as Isabelle struck up a friendship with Lucy, and moved in with her.

'I suppose they can comfort each other' thought June as she watched them from her window. They seemed happy in each other's company, walking and talking together. There were periods where June would join them, but the bond between the two heart sore girls was so strong, that friend number three felt like an outsider looking in and secretly envied the ability that, she perceived, they had, to love a boy so deeply and completely. The intensity they seemed to feel for their guys, made June feel that she was lacking in something very precious...what she saw in her childish way, as a mature love life.

This being said, Lucy's home life was not a happy one. She lived alone with her mother, who was an attractive woman with a habit of drinking too much. Her flat was dark and depressing with a permanent smell of alcohol in the air and the curtains were always drawn against the light. The solitary woman was a bit of an enigma, as she rarely left her room. Lucy would disappear into the bowels of darkness to converse with her and re-emerge, well provided with money to see her through the week. With a slam of the front door, she would shrug her depressing home life aside and bolt, like a little wild filly into the sunlight with her friends.

One sultry afternoon, Lucy and June decided to visit Isabelle in her new digs. It was hot and humid in the sun and it was safer, physically, to be indoors with others of like mind. The sporty type were happy to scorch their bodies out in the surf, but June was beginning to relate better to those who liked the shade during the hot season, Unfortunately the social group that preferred the shade also preferred some of the shadier activities as they squatted in their cool flats.

This particular apartment which June and Lucy were visiting, was unfortunately right next door to the local police station, which was a tricky situation for the tenants, who were teetering precariously close to the edge of getting arrested for the possession of illegal drugs. So, much care was taken to whom the door was opened. In this case, the door opened an inch and then wide enough to let the two girls in. Frank Zappa's raunchy voice filtered out from within.

It was Foxy's flat and he was quite happy to share it with all the kids in the street, especially to young run away girls, like Isabelle.

Like his name's sake, he had sharp features that resembled a fox and his hair fell into a flick on his forehead. His shirtless torso was muscular and his baggies sat precariously on his hips as he concentrated on punching holes in a leather belt.

Soon, Isabelle appeared from the back room wrapped in a sheet. A tall, heavy lidded man tagged behind her. They settled down on the big couch which was already holding the two girls. The sleepy man flung his arm, casually around the back of the sofa in the direction of Isabelle. He made it clear that it was only he, who had a claim on his cute, new toy. Remnants of leather lay on the rug and the coffee table was laden down with tools and half made sandals and belts.

In the centre of the room, a mound of freshly crushed 'grass', lay, piled up on a piece of newspaper. June had never seen so much marijuana in her life She had seen a few of the guys with 'joints' or small sticks wrapped in brown paper, but this was too much. She felt a bit uneasy and remembered the day when Rachel and her had experimented with a *slowboat* which was a cigarette rolled with marijuana. They had got so high, and lost all account of time, then they got the munchies and had to go to the shop to top up on their intake of fat-free crackers and in June's disorientated state, she nearly got run over by a car.

Having returned home, this time, without Rachel, she found that her mother had kindly made her bed while she had been out. On the pillow lay a small wad of weed, which the maker of the bed was sure to have seen. She was probably just waiting, in her indirect way of doing things, for a full confession from June.

'Its not what you think it is mum, really it isn't',' stammered June as she stumbled through to the lounge where she was doing the ironing. The girl stood there with the damning evidence between her fingers. Her mother looked bewildered, and it was then that the penny dropped... Mother had not even seen it and had no idea of what had been going on. But now she did...June deliberately blocked out what had happened after that, as it was not a pleasant memory.

Now she found herself in a similar situation but all the wiser. She would save her mother the trouble of punishing her. She wasn't going to cause her any more concern by clumsily confessing anything this time.

'Make it, make it...' croaked the young man who had, by this time successfully attached himself to Isabelle.

'You make it Mick...ek se, I'm busy here' answered Foxy seemingly resentful at the thought of sharing his cargo of dope with his hanger on friends, when it could get a good price on the streets. He resumed his work on the belt.

Mick reached out for the clay pipe which, in the shops, was sold as an incense holder.

'How's a mix' he said looking at Lucy, who always had a packet of Benson and Hedges in her bag. The pipe was subsequently stuffed with grass and tobacco, and before June knew it a lit pipe was being passed around. How could she say no to it. She really didn't want to get stoned, it was not a good experience for her, she did not enjoy the sensation, but to refuse would be so uncool, and these people *were* cool, she really wanted their friendship. She looked at Lucy and then again at Isabelle. How come they weren't having the same inner struggle that she was having? Perhaps they were really good at hiding their feelings....that she decided was 'cool' in itself.

Mick offered her the pipe and held it for her so that she could take a puff. June hesitated and looked into Mick's grey eyes, he did not wince but assumed simply that June was up for it.

'Oh to hell with it' thought June, 'I'm going to get stoned on the fumes anyway'. She took a puff and began coughing and spluttering. Micky looked amused and handed it to Lucy who grasped it in an experienced manner and took a pull and with no hesitation handed it on to Isabelle who repeated the act just as non-chalantly.

The repetitive sound of Frank Zappa's guitar gradually became more enjoyable and June felt like she understood his music at last. She sat quietly drinking it in, not daring to say anything or go anywhere lest she make a total idiot of herself. Her plan was to wait till the sensation wore off and then make her way home.

'Id really dig to get this grass wrapped, and wrapped quickly' said Foxy, not looking up from his work.

'We can't have the feds snooping around this pad, especially since the captain of the drug squad is supposed to be real sharp.'

'You mean Captain Van Wyk? Hey...he's a force to be reckoned with'. If he busted us, he would have us for breakfast!' answered Mick and let out a hearty laugh, that triggered a giggle from the girls.

'Hey Foxy, don't you have a camp coming up soon? Continued Micky

'Yeh, and I need to get these sticks out onto the streets before that...I really need the bread.'

'Don't stress, we'll smoke it for you, bro' continued Micky in a jovial manner.

The comment did not invoke any amusement on the leather maker's part, but on the contrary, the stamping process became more deliberate and heavy handed. An elaborate pattern was emerging from the soft leather and June found herself totally engrossed in the task.

It was late when June eventually returned home, she headed straight for the fridge to get a drink of water because she was so thirsty. She glimpsed at her reflection in the kettle and noted that her eyes were as red as traffic lights.

'Mum would surely become suspicious if she noticed that,' thought June.

'Perhaps I could pretend I've been crying or something' connived the little schemer.

To her surprise though, her mother seemed engrossed in something else, giving her the convenient opportunity to slip past her discerning eye. She eloped briskly into the privacy of her room, and didn't hesitate to wonder why she hadn't been pulled up to give an account of the evening's happenings. Not that the accounts were ever accurate.

64

Mother's pre-occupation was with her Dad at that particular moment. She lay in her bed looking into the darkness, still feeling light headed as if she was going to float away and a sudden feeling of nausea came over her. Intense conversation between her parents was raging in the lounge.

'what could they be on about?' Wondered June.

She had never heard them speak a harsh word to each other and it was a new experience to hear her mother so distressed.

'Roy, I won't have you coming home in this condition again.....this drinking has to stop......if it doesn't.....' there was a pause.

'June and I are leaving this God-forsaken place and going back to England.....You hear me!'

There was a sound of footsteps and the bedroom door closed. Then there was silence.

Her dad had been spending more and more time at his ski boat club where he owned a motor boat and frequently went deep sea fishing with his mates. June went along a few times and got burnt to a cinder in the merciless sun. She had, though, after being strapped into her seat, caught a really big fish, much to the admiration of all her dad's mates, but all these happy memories did not justify the fact that her dad was spending longer and longer hours drinking with his fishermen friends. He was reminded often by his adamant wife that the 'only reason that we are in this country, is so that *you* can go fishing!'...mother's emphasis on the word *'you'* had a cutting edge for special effects.

She could not imagine life without her dad and the thought of it was dreadful. He was so adventurous and it was this trait in him that led him to Africa in the first place. Her very first memories alluded to times with her dad and his friends, in the African bush, returning home from a day out hunting for game, with guinea fowl for dinner and Jack the bird dog, proudly prancing along at their side. So many happy memories with her daddy could not end in such a way. Separation would be too horrid to comprehend.

She closed her eyes and tried to sleep but images of her friends came before her, Bugsy ...he didn't have an easy life. His dad used to beat his mum and sometimes the young boy had to get in the middle of the fight and try and stop the blows that were meant for his mother.

Ken, once went on holiday with his dad, but because it started to rain they came home the same day, and that was the boy's only memory of a holiday with his meagre family unit. So many of her friends didn't even know *their* dads. Faces drifted into June's mind and as she pondered on each one's plight, she fell into a troubled sleep.

CHAPTER 11

'Its the wrong time, the wrong place
The wrong way for me.'
Spooky Tooth 1969

Perhaps it was the adventurous spirit that she had inherited from her dad or maybe it was just plain naughtiness. Whatever it was, June had to admit that school was dreadfully boring and so, to help her through the day, she would get up to all sorts of mischief with her friends.

She especially despised the daily interrogation that took place in the mornings before assembly. The girls had to walk past the deputy head, Miss Wallace, single file, and endure her meticulous attention on things like the length of the girls' skirts, nails, and fringes. Attention was taken on details such as do the girls' have makeup or nail varnish on? There were also occasions where the little woman would call a girl aside to see if she was wearing respectable knickers! On this particular occasion the wiry little tyrant noticed a glimmer of a gold crucifix peaking out of June's shirt collar.

'You, young lady, come here!' she screeched, June left the line to stand before the little dictator.

'Remove that jewellery instantly!' she commanded.

'No Miss' came the startling retort. There was a tense silence as the girls turned to take note of the conflict that was sure to follow.

'How dare you talk back to me in that manner!' Snapped the astonished woman.

A brief battle of the wills ensued, and then June launched into a tall, but touching tale about an imaginery friend who was killed in a road accident minutes after he gave her the necklace. To make it more believable June rambled on about how she had seen the whole tragic incident and had been traumatised by it. Therefore, she would *not* remove the necklace.

To the surprise of her large audience, Miss Wallace, the one who never showed mercy to any of the girls, believed the story that had not even a fragment of truth in it. With misty eyes she dismissed June with uncharacteristic tenderness. June turned on her heels, her eyes sparkled with mischief just about as much as the glint from the necklace which still hung around her neck.

'You should write fiction novels,' giggled the girls

' Miss *"Walrus Face"* has never yielded to such rubbish before!' laughed one of the senior girls' as she glided past in the opposite direction.

By the time June reached her junior exams her little crew of friends had whittled away completely, except for Rachel who remained a loyal comrade to the end of her mundane experience at a state school.

Celeste had got married after discovering that she was pregnant and Sammy had gone to Australia. The others had been scattered about amongst the other classes. Rachel, who was much more docile and determined to endure the boredom, had one objective and that was to get a qualification which would see her able to take over her dad's business in the future. She continued to plod along in the everyday humiliations of a state school system, but eventually even she could not face another boring day of it.

So, after a period of desperate brain storming, the two of them stumbled upon the brilliant idea of applying to finish school at a private institution, where there were lots of boys and very few rules and regulations. It did not take too much effort, convincing June's mother of the great benefits of the private school system and she bought the idea avidly. 'Buying' was definitely the operative word, because it would certainly empty her parents' already meagre bank account.

In an odd sort of way, June sensed that her mother was secretly relieved that she did not have to face the humiliating prospect of, possibly seeing her daughter being expelled from school. This was as good a solution as any, although it was an expensive one as well.

---oOo---

The ominous warning that June's father had received from her resolute mother yielded successful results, because he spent much more time at home, following that night of threats. After dinner it was his habit to sit in his favourite chair with his newspaper, just like it was before he had hit a 'wobbly' as June had called it.

He was conveniently available to answer all June's questions, which were coming fast and furiously since being introduced to her new English teacher at her fancy school. Her English teacher, Mr. Scott, was a member of the United Party which was the opposition party to the present Nationalist government. He was dangerously vocal about what he believed and his class of students were just a fragment of his sizeable audience which he was gathering around him. In one of those unforgettable English lessons, which had turned into a political debate, June had raised her hand to ask what the [xii]Sharpesville riots were. An uneasy silence followed at which a pin could have been heard dropping, and then a corporate sigh arose from the students, who expressed relief, that they had not been so idiotic with their choice of question.

'Miss Paine!' came the reply, 'You mean to say you have never heard of that fateful day when men, women and children were killed during the riots of 1960?'

She squirmed uncomfortably in her seat and all her peers turned to look at her accusingly, each secretly conscious of their own unawareness of the true unrest in the country.

On the other hand her dad's take on the same issue was 'We don't want the Communists here!', which left June a little puzzled as she could not quite see how the Communists fitted into the picture, but then again her dad was always right, or perhaps 'right wing' was the more correct phrase.

It was on one of these nights that discussion had ended in the conclusion that the Communists would be kept out of the country at all costs, when a terrible blood curdling scream ascended from the ground floor of the building.

June's mother ran out doors to the back stairs and June followed on her heels.

'What is it mum?' she asked as she looked into her mum's colourless face, and then followed her gaze down to the ground floor of the building where, on the cold, hard concrete lay the lifeless form of a little girl. They could only look helplessly on, as the anguished parents gathered up the limp, little body, who had fallen fourteen floors to her death. The seconds felt like hours as the sound of grief stricken cries echoed around the building. At last, two people stepped out of the darkness and embraced the distraught couple, consoling them gently.

'Who would have the courage to enter such a circle of anguish and pain.' thought June. She strained her eyes to see who the comforters were and recognized the lady with the long black hair and her husband. They had been the youth leaders from the coffee bar who she had tried to avoid, the night Lucy and her had run off to Wind and Sea. Suddenly June felt remorse for the way she had behaved that night, after all she could have at least shown a little more respect.

'I suppose it's only natural that it would be Christians who would show courage enough to approach such a traumatic scene. Who else would have the boldness to venture into such a space? Thank goodness they were there to help.' She mused, as she turned away from the tragic event and retreated back inside where her familiar surroundings made her feel safe.

The thought of that little girl lying like a tiny rag doll, her blond hair framing her cherub like face caused June to withdraw quietly into her room to think about her life afresh. She brooded over the state of the young couple. How would they ever get over such a terrible experience of losing their first born child in such a tragic way?

She decided that high rise buildings were a terrible hazard. She had heard a story about a girl named Mary, It had not meant much to her at the time, as she only knew her by sight, but now after seeing what had just happened she thought about the incident again. Mary had tried to climb through the window of her flat, after having a fight with her boyfriend who had locked her out. The hitch was that between the wall that she was balancing on and the kitchen window, was a 15 floor drop. Being a little tipsy she had stumbled and slipped to her death all those floors below

'She was just a young girl, how could such a terrible thing have happened?' mused June, as she sat cross legged on her bed staring into space. After removing an over full ash tray, she rummaged through some comics and magazines until she eventually found her Bible. She flicked through the pages and realized that she had neglected her resolution of reading a chapter every day. She felt such a failure, what was the use of starting now. She snapped the book closed and stretched out on her bed, wondering what the future held for her and when would be her time to die, the gloom remained throughout the night.

CHAPTER 12

"goin' up the country, gotta get away,
well, I'm goin' some place that I've never been
before." Canned Heat 1969

In the morning June dragged herself off to college. The gloom had lifted slightly, at the thought of the holidays, which were only a week away. Simon the youth leader from 'Life Beat' had talked her into going to a Christian camp during the holidays. Her first reaction had been a reluctant and resigned 'yeah ok' but now suddenly, she felt that actually this would be the *right* thing to do.

A dull, flat feeling had lingered with her through the night and she was feeling drained from lack of sleep. She hoped that the decision she had made to go along was the right one. To be surrounded by Christians would help her to overcome her fears. Pulling deeply on her first cigarette of the day, she handed it to Rachel as usual. Rachel prided herself on the fact that she didn't smoke, but annoyingly expected at least a few puffs of every cigarette that June lit.

How she was going to face the day was a challenge. She just wasn't up for being drilled by Mr. Scott, who felt it his task to instil the idea in his student's heads that if they didn't pass their exams they might as well commit suicide. Why he had to be so mellow dramatic when giving his students pep talks was beyond June's comprehension, especially since it was his habit to deviate so far from the curriculum. A heated political debate would usually be the outcome of the lesson and June was sure that the poets would turn in their graves if they could hear Mr. Scott quoting them... but, oh so out of context!

---000---

The day finally arrived and June found herself part of a youth group, somewhere in the Eastern Transvaal. Simon had assured her that she would soon make friends and have a nice time, but she wasn't so sure about that, since the only people she knew was Simon and the senior girl from school who had sung at the coffee bar. The one that she had vowed to avoid at all costs, she remembered. It turned out that her name was Sue and she was quite nice after all.

It only took a day and a half for June to realize that all the sitting around listening to bible studies was not for her, in her head she had signed up for a holiday and a holiday was what she was going to get! The proverbial round peg in a square hole suited the restless girl and the rustling sound of the wind blowing through the branches of the great broom trees and the sparkling river at the bottom of the camp ground, triggered June's adventurous nature. Her heart was drawn towards the beautiful landscape of the Eastern Transvaal, where the grass was the colour of a lion's coat, and the sunsets were cast against the thorn trees on the plain. It was all too much... the temptation was too great and so, she soon rounded up a group of likeminded youngsters who, rather than listening to the droning on of a boring sermon found it more fun to go exploring, by firstly, having a wade in the river.

The fun was short lived as the half naked juveniles, after a long search, were discovered and bustled back to camp to face the penalty for their disobedience. June, being the ring leader, conveniently found Sue to be sympathetic towards her plight and she wept in her arms hoping to find protection from the coming consequences, that of an interview with the great inquisitor, the overseer of the youth camp, who was in his mid fifties.

'What you have done is not acceptable.' He began. 'I have a good mind to send you home'. He continued in his broad, Dutch accent.

'Oh no, please sir, give me another chance'. implored June.

I will give you another chance on these conditions'.

What are they Sir.?'

'Firstly you have to stop that disgusting habit of smoking.'

Yes, Sir' answered June, wondering how on earth she was going to kick the habit, especially since she had packed a whole carton of cigarettes.

'Secondly,' he continued, 'You will have to take off those false eyelashes that you insist on wearing.'

But they're not false S....'

He interjected rudely

'and as for that dirty striped shirt that you are wearing.....well change it!'

'but Sir its not dirty its beige!' retorted June, genuinely annoyed at the man's ignorance of the latest fashion statements.

Without doubt, the man was in no mood to listen to trivia. His aim was to see a change in this kid, and it better be quick!

The harassed girl, suddenly felt very different from all the other youngsters who, under pressure, reverted back to their former conventional selves, which only added to her feeling of aloneness. Her only option was to change or be sent home to disappoint her mother once again. This was a formidable task. She wished that there was some sort of instruction book that she could turn to.   How could she be someone that she wasn't?

She looked in the mirror and began to wipe all her make-up off.   Rummaging through her suitcase, she realized that in it, was nothing appropriate to wear. Her crop tops, serongs and levi jeans were not acceptable here. In a panic she grabbed her carton of cigarettes and dug a big hole out the back of the prefabs, and covered the twenty packets of cigarettes over with soft soil, vowing that she would never smoke again.

That night presented a very different looking June, thanks to Sue who conjured up a pure white outfit for her and presented her, proudly, to the leadership. No one was convinced of the change and least of all was June. So early in the morning she dug up her carton of cigarettes and admitted defeat to everyone. This was followed by a cheerful team leader, who seemed relieved to leave the youth camp early, to escort her back home. Once again, she would have to offer some sort of explanation to her mum.

'Poor mum,' she thought gazing out of the train window, as the dry landscape of the Transvaal gradually gave way to the green hills of Natal. She just couldn't face her mother's shock and disappointment again.

It all came back to her, how she had been escorted home the last time. It had been from school, by a social worker. Her mother was, as predicted, alarmed to say the least. The social worker apologised for the muddle up. But after listening to the story mother exclaimed.

'This is not a muddle, this is a meddle!'

It had been, that a suspicious spectator, peering from a balcony high up in a building had noticed the daily gathering in the park, of school kids having their first cigarette of the day. The over imaginative observer who obviously had nothing better to do, had jumped to the conclusion that something very sinister was going on and had subsequently reported it.

So, when June arrived at school, she was arrested by the seniors and whisked off to Miss Roberts, the head teacher.

'You are here because it's been reported that you have been smoking marijuana in the park before school.' Announced the little woman behind the big desk. June looked genuinely confused, and shrugged her shoulders in bewilderment.

'Well answer me, have you been taking drugs in the park with your friends?'

'No Miss' came the answer

Miss Roberts addressed the prefect who had escorted June into the office.

'Search her sandwiches!' she demanded, pointing with her bony finger at June's satchel.

The prefect was puzzled at the order given her and hesitated for a moment.

'I said search her sandwiches!'

She sighed resignedly and with reluctance, rummaged half heartedly through June's satchel, until she found a little parcel wrapped lovingly, by her mother, in rice paper. She opened up the parcel and began pulling the sandwiches apart, frowning at the smell of boiled egg which filled the room and also wondering why she had ever accepted the so-called, prestigious position of being a prefect.

These were the famous sandwiches that were fought over by June's friends, they were renown for being delicious and June bartered with them relentlessly. She traded them every day for a vanilla slice and other tasty things that delighted her palette but now, regretfully, there they lay in pieces. The not so wholesome smell permeated every corner of the Head teacher's office.

Miss Roberts looked a little sheepish, and was not sure what to do next. Admitting defeat was out of the question, she reasoned that there must be something dark, driving this troubled young soul. So, she contacted social services and had June taken home by a social worker.

'Poor mum' mused June once again, as she became conscious that the click clack of the train had come to a halt and they had reached their destination.

She shuffled through to her room, dishevelled and silent, dragging her bag behind her and her parents felt that, to give her space, would be the wisest thing.

June could not be humoured. She was too angry. Angry that she had even consented to go along to such a camp full of 'aliens' as she called them. There was no possibility of being part of that clique and she promised herself to stay well away from those holy Joes in the future.

'If it hadn't been for Sue who accepted me as I am, I would say that all Christians are not worth the time of day.' She relayed back to her mother, who made herself at home on June's bed and lit a cigarette for the two of them.

Her mother crossed her legs and cupped her head in her hand as she pondered her daughter's latest views on life.

'You know, Mum, I think I hate Christians.' Said June with conviction.

'Oh Darling, don't talk like that, you *know* that you are one.' Answered her mother, after a brief pause.

'How do you know that mum, what would you say if I said that I wasn't'

'Oh don't be silly love, you're British aren't you!' she continued, elegantly releasing a swirl of white smoke from her pink lips.

'But that doesn't make me a Christian!'

'Well it doesn't make you a Muslim either, now come and have your lunch!' she replied non chalantly, stubbing her cigarette out in an already over loaded ash tray.

June was hungry, and followed her mother to the table. She toyed with her bacon and eggs quietly, wondering what that conversation was all about, trying to work out how being British had anything to do with being a Christian. She could not quite make head or tail of it except that her mum had been brought up in the Sudan, where Arabs were Muslim and British colonials were so-called Christians and the native Sudanese were caught in between. Surely there was more to it than that though? Sue seemed to possess something deeper and more personal than that external religion that was all bound up in nationality. She wanted what Sue had or nothing at all.

'Most of them were just hypocrites' she ruminated, as she chewed her food more thoughtfully than usual.

CHAPTER 13

'Excuse me while I kiss the sky'
Jimi Hendrix 1967

It was September 1970, Jimi Hendrix had died of an overdose. June was with her friends at Andy's place when the news was heard. Andy had just finished one of the gruelling army camps, and was still in the habit of going everywhere in his trench coat, slept with his boots on and for some unknown reason felt that raw eggs were a sustaining diet for him. This caused him, at sporadic moments, during the day to take a raw egg out of his coat pocket, crack it open into his mouth and swallow the slimey contents with one gulp. It always bothered June that, one day, he would retrieve one big eggie mess from the bowels of his coat pocket, but surprisingly that never seemed to happen.

He insisted on listening to Noddy records while driving around in his Beetle, and it was on this particular night that he rounded everybody up and packed them all into the car, with the intention of spending the night at 'Peace park' where he planned to commemorate the death of his great idol, by consuming a couple of bottles of wine and a few 'slowboats' with his mates .

June was keen to go along as she was fascinated by the transformation of her childhood friend, Bobby, who she had not seen for at least two years. Bobby had shot up like a supple young bean stalk and now looked down on everyone with his hair flopping around his face. His brown, almond shaped eyes, were a bit squint and the truth was, that he offended everyone by ignoring them, only because he desperately needed specs, but his warm, catchy laugh, invoked pardon from all. He curled himself up into a little ball and endured the trip to the park.

'We'll spend half the night at Peace Park and then we'll go and watch the sun rise over the sea.' Andy declared as he pulled up at the petrol station.

'Hey Baba,' he shouted to the petrol attendant, 'give us fifteen Rand's worth' The petrol attendant sprinted up to the overloaded beetle, smiling from ear to ear and began to fill the car with petrol.

'I don't think I'll be in any condition to watch the sun rise', chuckled Bugsy as he tried to shift his legs into a more comfortable position. The petrol attendant replaced the nossel and took the twenty Rand note from Andy.

That's what we're doing, we'll be high and it will be a blast' answered Andy dictatorially. He cupped his hand out the window as he waited for his change.

The petrol attendant shuffled frantically through his overalls, and searched each pocket for change.

'Sorry Bass' he finally said and threw his hands up, shrugging melodramatically. His expressive brown eyes glinted with mischief and a smile swept across his black moon shaped face.

'No change? I suppose, you never have change! What's wrong with you people!' Shouted Andy. He revved up his car and pulled off at full speed, as fast as a Beetle could go.

'[xiii]Ya bonga bass, Yabonga' shouted the petrol attendant after him, waving cheerfully, as Andy sped around the corner, causing his tyres to screech.

To everyone's relief the trip didn't take too long. The doors flung open and seven people spilled out of the bubble car. The moonlight shone upon the thin tree trunks which took on a life of their own as they swayed around like anoerexic ghosts. This was a perfect place to express their grief over the decease of the life of Jimi Hendrix. They settled down to listen to his brilliant guitar solos and June edged closer to Bobby's side, where she hoped to remain for the night.

'Gee June you've changed' he whispered

'You too', came the reply as June slipped her arm through his.

'Just like old times, hey'. He giggled, his laugh infectious enough to invite the response from those around him. He dropped June's arm gently down as he fished through his pockets for something that seemed quite important to him and pulled out a piece of folded silver paper. June wondered why she was competing with a piece of candy for his attention. He unwrapped it carefully, and called for a razor blade and a record cover. He spoke softly to June, aware that it was important to keep her attentive to his person, but the tiny article was the centre of attention, as he meticulously halved it, then quartered it, then quartered it again.

'What is that?' she asked, in a child like manner. Bobby glanced in surprise at her.

'This.....,' he said, 'is the sweetest slice of *Purple Haze* that you could ever wish to have.'

He carefully resumed the operation, and added 'We're taking more than just a trip to Peace park tonight'. He bellowed heartily, as he passed the quartered cap of LSD around to the boys and then licked the record cover, making sure that not a speck was lost.

A dog barked in the distance as they lay down on blankets and looked up at the sky. There was a full moon and the air was warm. The frogs and crickets began their chorus again, once they realized that the little band of people were harmless. Gradually a large choir of invisible insects hummed all around them, harmoniously chanting in unison. 'om mani padme hum...om mani padme hum...it reminded June of the mantra of the Tibetan monks that she had been reading about as of late. Even the tiniest insect knew how to get in contact with the universe, reflected June.

The moment was suddenly broken.

'You know we're probably surrounded by poisonous snakes' Bugsy whispered, loud enough for all to hear. Alan turned up the music. The wow wow pedal was not that of the deceased artist, who seemed to have already been forgotten. But rather the band Mae Blitz had become the favouite and was belting out the rhythmic sound. Andy had settled himself comfortably into his sleeping bag and was enjoying his trip on LSD and was in no mood to accept a thought that could jeopardise his current peaceful frame of mind.

'You mean *mambas*' added June.

'yeh, green ones, black ones' answered Bugsy

'psychadelic!' giggled Jeannie.

Peter was new to the group and had come along for the squashed ride. He was leaning up against the beetle, rolling a slowboat.

'I bet none of you have even seen a mamba...in the army, I killed one' he boasted.

'Oh yes! Me too!' replied June, excitedly. She had forgotten that the boys were starting to get high on LSD and that she was a fairly good story teller.

'When I was little, once when we were on holiday in Mombasa, my dad heard a rustling under the bed and it was a really long black mamba, he killed it. They used to get up into the thatched rooves and drop down....wahh' she shivered for special effect...'you should just see the photo of my dad holding the thing...its the same size as him.!'

By this time everyone had deliberately switched off and were focusing on the music. The sound of the *wow wow* pedal blotted out all the other sounds.

The stars were twinkling brightly.

'look at those' said Annie

as she pointed romantically up at the stars. She had sidled up close to Pete, who had now reclined on a blanket with her.

'Hey Space Kids! who's up for checking around our camp to make sure there's no snakes?' exclaimed Andy, who had not been able to erase the vision of the snakes from his potentially, delusional frame of mind.

He was now as high as a kite, but seemed to be keeping a handle on things even though he had braced himself for the prospect of snakes dropping down on him from the trees.

'Go on Pete, you seem to know all about it...get my [xiv]sjambok out of the car and go a looking'.

Pete rose reluctantly. He wished that he had kept his big trap shut but he had to impress Annie. He sighed and picked up the sjambok and disappeared among the trees.

Unfortunately the tow rope was hanging out of the boot of the car. Bugsy had already gravitated over towards the car, feeling a little safer, by being near it, if he needed to make a quick escape. Playfully he reached for the rope and threw it out in front of him. It looked quite cool there in the grass. He began to pull it back slowly admiring the way it moved.

The reaction was immediate. The girls scrambled to their feet screaming at the top of their voices. The boys took flight. Pete appeared with his sjambok and began frantically whipping the piece of rope that was still moving through the grass with Bugsy at the other end, reeling it in. At this point, Bugsy got a fright and retreated inside the car for protection from his friends who had visibly gone mad.   Gradually the penny dropped....

'It's only a rope' stammered Jeanie in a thin voice, laughing nervously.

Bobby burst into uncontrollable laughter, at which everyone followed suit. With a sigh of relief everyone settled back down again and resumed their former activities.

The flustered six agreed that Bugsy was best restrained inside the car. He agreed with their decision as well and fell asleep in the front seat.

'What has happened to my hand brake!', shouted Andy, when dawn was upon them. He shook Bugsy awake and waved the broken hand brake in his face. Bugsy opened one eye, to see the ripped wires waving in his face. For a moment he couldn't remember.

'Oh yes, now I remember...real sorry...I thought it was a snake and I must have ripped it out of the socket.'

At this Bugsy was banished to the very back of the car and Andy did not talk to him for the rest of the day.

They drove back to the beach.   The sky was crimson, as the sun rose over the sea.

[xv]'U yangi thanda n'Kulu Kulu' the black workmen dressed in blue overalls, sang melodiously, as they hurled their axes in unison into the tar and worked on the roads.

Although there had been a few hiccups with the evening, Peace Park had been true to its name and things had worked out peacefully.

'Phew! thank goodness for that.' Sighed June. 'It had been a good night.'

CHAPTER 14

'My soul stretched tight across the sky
To fade behind a city block'
T.S. Eliot 'Preludes'

Lieu was a friend of Bobby's. This was not his real name, although it could've been. The secret was in the spelling. It had been given to him by his peers at boarding school, because he was regularly caned on his backside leaving red welts that looked like stripes, thus his name, *Lieutenant.* He took a shine to June almost immediately. June was not sure what Lieu's day job was but she was very aware of what he did at night, he was the runner for a rock band. His job was to load and unload the band's equipment. It was more of a hobby to him than actually a job and he enjoyed all the attention which he received, as he was often mistaken for one of the band. This was a great bonus because it mean't that he had the world at his finger tips, namely sex, drugs, and rock and roll. The members of the band were brothers and looked just the part. They had thick manes of black, curly hair and their rugged faces were deliberately unshaved for three days at a time. They looked quite rough to their adoring fans, yet, in reality they were just big soft teddies, because their sensitivity to all things moral only directed them back to their staunch, Greek parents, whose strong set of values, went back through several generations.

Saturday nights began to follow a pattern, as June tagged along with her boyfriend and his beloved band from gig to gig. The night club, *Wind and Sea*, which previously was the hangout for all things to do with the surfing community and underground music, had evolved and adopted a new name, *Mumbles*, which was a suitable label and reflected the image of the club that was getting progressively darker in reputation.

Much to their surprise, the band found that they were in demand at this dingy but popular night club . Lieu reminded them that 'they jammed like Eric Clapton'. What a great honour to be compared with a *cat* like Eric Clapton!

With these words of encouragement, for obviously that is what Lieu was good at...encouraging... June had decided, the band pressed on with their jam sessions, keeping their noses on the job at hand, only sporadically, peering through their curls at the occasional pretty face.

Lieu's schedule included fuelling the brothers with motivational pep talks about their talented musical abilities but this did not stop at flattery. He also provided them with a cocktail of drugs to keep them on the road. Their doting mother, who was ever present in their minds, was blissfully unaware of such vices, and was under the impression that they were performing at some illustrious club only fit for the likes of her boys. June often wondered what she would have done if she had known where her boys were performing and how they were able to keep playing all night long. The answer lay in the fact that Lieu diligently found ways to keep them permanently stoked up and fuelled with drugs, even if it meant going downstairs to pick up heads of the marijuana from the gutters, to smoke later on in the evening.

Mumbles was frequently raided by the drug squad and the raids would take place at the most unexpected times, because of this and for fear that the club would be closed down, the organisers encouraged their clients to search the gutters around the club for heads of marijuana, so that there would be no evidence of the activities taking place. Lieu did not need much prompting to perform the job, hence, he took on the responsibility for the club manager.

***

'Damn, I left my pipe at home!' cursed Lieu, as he walked home with June, after a gig. He searched through the pockets of his military waste coat. 'Do you have one?' he said, addressing Bobby and his friend, whose little fox terrier followed close at their heels. Lieu was visibly annoyed with himself.
Bobby shook his head, but spotted a glass bottle on the pavement.

'We'll have to use a bottle neck' he replied as he picked it up and smacked it against the corner of a wall. The bottle shattered, leaving only the neck intact. June was intrigued at her friend's ability to improvise if he had to and even if it was a sign that he had become addicted to the weed, she told herself that he was marvellous.

They came to a small park surrounded by buildings and squatted behind a clump of trees. It was dark and the little company felt safe, being sure that they would not be seen. They reasoned that it was better to smoke their gleanings from the gutter then and there, because, as Leiu put it,

'the feds were out in full force tonight.'

June made herself comfortable on a rock. The smoke from the bottle neck swirled into the sky and she followed its trail up through the gap between the buildings, into the dark stillness of the night.

Although the stars could not be seen clearly, because of the city lights, it still conjured up feelings that she wanted to fly away, as far away as the furthest galaxy. She was already bored with the weekly routine, and yawned with disinterest. Lazily, the sleepy girl looked around at all the buildings which loomed above her. Lights glinted from each little apartment. They were like little boxes...lots of little boxes. A different story to be told in each, yet the same final ending.

'We live out our futile lives....for what? One minute we're here and then we're gone...what's the point.?' She wondered with jaded cynicism.

The little dog trotted over to her side and wagged his docked tail, she patted him gently and continued to reflect on the lives of people like Lieu's mother, who was a widow. Her struggles of being a single mum with a full time job and never enough money to do anything meaningful, was the fate of most of the women in the community.

Feeling grossly depressed at her own pessimistic views, a swathe of desire came over her to take a puff of the weed to dull the senses, perhaps it would put her in a better frame of mind and block out the ever present, unanswerable questions knocking around in her head. On the contrary, she decided, eventually, there was no point in numbing herself. The sensation didn't appeal to her anyway. Just to find something that could help her to escape the meaninglessness of life, a stimulating incentive, an inspiration to guide her life.....that would suffice.

'Cat, come over here boy' Bobby's friend, whose nickname was Buzz, whistled gently and summoned his little dog to him and blew a puff of smoke into his face. 'Cat' sat at his feet and wavered slightly from side to side, getting thoroughly intoxicated on the fumes.

At that moment the young man caught June's eye and he could not help but notice the look of disapproval that swept across her face momentarily. She tried to hide her feelings, and thought that perhaps she should strike up a conversation about his name and its origin.

That was always a good ice breaker, but it was so obvious. ...He was permanently buzzing out on drugs and to be honest, she was in no mood for light talk anyway. If it wasn't for Bobby, she would have made tracks home on her own a long time ago.

Buzz looked a little embarrassed and flippantly said,

'My dog's a *cool cat* really, that's why his name is "Cat".'

Well that answered that unprovoked question she thought and sighed with boredom.

His comment caused him to laugh a little too loudly for June's liking. She smiled weakly at him.

Although his actions had not been to June's approval, she was thankful for being distracted from her thoughts.

'I've been called up' said Bobby glumly looking into the embers of the pipe.

'Safe my Broer, you'll be cool,' replied the older man, Lieu.

'Just ^{xvi}vasbyte my broer, you'll be cool.' He repeated himself, yet, with less conviction.

'Do what the ^{xvii}Larnies tell you to and get it over and done with.' Came the next instruction.

'I've been assigned to the infantry'.

'Hey... infantry, my broer that's cannon fodder ^{xviii}speel!' interjected Buzz chortling under his breath.

'How would you know my friend, you've been spared the hell?' came the reply from the lighter skinned man.

'^{xix}Yeh, only because I was born on the wrong side of the colour spectrum' continued Buzz and he chuckled some more. 'If I had one of your rifles, I would shoot them all!' There was a poignant silence.

'The system is corrupt.' Continued Bobby,

'and now I have to go and fight for it...hey I think I'm going to ^{xx}*Awol*, before I even start.' Bobby's voice quavered slightly.

Lieu grabbed hold of Bobby's sleeve.

'Hey broer, no, the MP's will bust you.....they'll put you away. If you want my advice, just grin and bear it...Look at those ^{xxi}Jehovah Witnesses they spend two years in the clink... now you don't want that do you?'

Bobby looked at his fist clutching the bottle neck and realized that the embers had died. He tapped it on the ground and the last of the ashes dropped out.

'And remember' added Lieu in a fatherly manner 'Be careful of the ^{xxii}zol in Angola, some have mistook ^{xxiii}*Malpitte* for good stuff. That dope, will make you go mad...Just a warning, son.'

Bobby looked apprehensively at Lieu. His brown eyes, glazed with a crimson sheen, gave the appearance of a little boy who had been crying.

'Perhaps he was crying....crying inside' thought June, remembering things Bobby had told her about his boyhood. His dad was from Afrikaaner stock and his mother was Malaysian.

'That's why he's so pretty' she thought as she studied him, but his life had not been pretty. His father, in drunken stupors had beaten him up often, as a child, and out of spite had kidnapped his older brother, never to be seen again. It was all so debilitating.

At that moment, one of the balconies in a nearby building lit up suddenly and a silhouette appeared. A man bellowed at the top of his voice.

'I know you're out there and I've called the police. They're coming to get you!'

Seized by alarm, Lieu took June by the hand and ran. Buzz quickly grabbed his little dog and bolted with him in the crook of his arm, and Bobby was close behind. They ran, until they could not run anymore.

Like pigeons, they took flight. Not stopping to think, that perhaps it was a practical joker getting some paranoid kids fleeing for their lives.

In between the panting from exhaustion, Lieu kissed June at her front door, and after a very brief farewell, she stepped quickly inside, with the intent of terminating the relationship as soon as possible.

It was not necessary that her flustered state had to be explained to her mother, who stood at the door to welcome her dishevelled daughter home. A censored version of the night's happenings would suffice for the woman's curious ears, determined June, as she launched into her usual expose of the nights happenings, keeping under wraps the 'running away like rats' episode.

CHAPTER 15

How many Roads must a man walk down
Before you can call him a man?
Bob Dylan 1965

The 350 cc Scrambler motor bike speeded up the sand dune at full throttle, its back wheel wavering from side to side, while Champ's thick leather boot steadied it till it reached the top.   Everyone applauded from the bottom of the sandy hill.

Then it was Henry on his smaller 175cc that attempted the ascent. With more success the lighter bike ascended to the peak at a quicker pace. The applauding company set the stop watch again for the next hopeful rider. Bobby appeared on his 50cc, although a bit of an anti climax, the amused audience continued to cheer and clap and were relieved that the bike was only little when it came plummeting back down with rider in tow, causing an avalanche of sand which tumbled down to the foot of the dune, from which Bobby emerged, grinning from ear to ear.

It was a grand afternoon! The girls were especially pleased with the latest developments, that of boys on motorbikes. What a great combination, not only for some fun, but also for a means of transport to get to places that were usually unattainable except by hitch hiking. June and her friends had done their fair share of that and at times it had got quite nerve wracking and dangerous to say the least. She had deliberately repressed the memory of being offered a lift from a stranger who took her and Lucy to an isolated place to show them pornographic pictures, the attempt to groom two young girls for a future in pornography backfired as the two of them escaped from the pervert and decided to walk the few miles. They were relieved for several reasons, when they eventually got to their destination that day.

Then there was the day that a big, shiney, but familiar Chevrolet, pulled up along the road and it turned out to be June's Dad! Sheepishly she got into the car with her friends, sadly aware that the fun of hitch hiking would be irreparably damaged after that.

But now! Here was a marvellous thing, lots of boys on motor bikes ready to lift the girls wherever they wanted to go. The only problem that the girls had with their new form of transport was how to cope with their tangled mass of hair, which needed sorting out when they reached their destinations. Hence the balaclava became a trend setter. The boys and girls tucked their long hair into the useful accessory before they zoomed off at full speed. The hoodlums would dice each other when the traffic lights turned green and impress the nerve wracked pedestrians with performances of high

94

flying [xxiv]*wheelies* , as they fled the scene like masked bank robbers.

Because Champ had the biggest bike he always tended to be the leader of the pack. He was not nicknamed Champ because he was a sporting champion, but rather, it was because he had been part of the military elite who were parachuted out of aeroplanes. June was a bit dubious about this fact as the stark evidence of him having bad eyesight, was obvious by the thick spectacles which he wore, this alone would have disqualified him from the platoon. But he was big and athletic and all the lads admired him, so it must've been true that he was a so-called parabat.

His athletic prowess was demonstrated one day, when the group decided to stop off at a popular spot to smoke some *pot* and do a bit of jamming on Bugsy's guitar. It was a new spot that had been discovered and the question of its function in the past was best left unanswered, although rumour had it, that it was once a sewer.

It was the perfect secret place because it was underground, dark and cool. One had to climb down a long, vertical ladder to get to the bottom. There was a small slit of light at the far end of the large tunnel which led onto the road outside and it seemed natural to settle down underneath the overhead, tiny window, and huddle together, passing cigarettes and [xxv]*slowboats* around, while Bugsy picked the strings on his guitar, weaving a simple tune one string at a time.

June meanwhile, lay her head on his shoulder and shut her eyes imagining that he was Bob Dylan. In the distance, a solitary silhouette approached them. It was Seth.

'Howzit, howzit!' he growled softly, as he stood over the reposed, shadowed figures. He scanned the landscape with one long glance and took note that it was safe to speak and then said

'A cargo of acid has arrived. Who wants?'

Feeling slightly exposed to the elements, he crouched down, so that he could have direct eye contact with those who were interested and even in the dull light, June noticed his piercing blue eyes, darting from person to person.

What type of Acid?' answered Champ casually,

Seth paused for a moment. 'Strawberry Fields'.

'Hmm that's a good Acid' purred Champ,

'Yeh, that sounds cool.'

'Count me in' piped up Brent, and then a few others affirmed their order.

The only one there, who represented the feminine gender, lifted her head from the guitarist's shoulder and asked the inevitable question that was on the silent lips of all of her kind.

'How is Luke?' Seth shuffled himself around to check out who was speaking to him.

'not good' he answered slowly. 'The shrinks have just given him another series of shock treatment......but it aint working, he's like a vegetable.

'When are they going to release him?' inquired June with concern in her voice. The girl's freckly brow creased accordingly.

Seth shook his head. 'Its like they've thrown the key away or something.....my broer ....hey he was a good oe .'

It was clear that Seth had thrown away the key of hope, the way he spoke of his brother in the past tense, thought June as she continued to gaze on Seth's handsome face, which obviously ran in the family. She had to admit though, that he was not as handsome or as charming as his younger brother.

Shrugging off the disturbing subject, he shifted his position in the direction of Champ, and did not take his eyes off his handy work, that of rolling a slowboat.

'Howzit going in the [xxvi]*Paras*?'

Champ kicked some damp soil away from him with his army boot and smiled. 'That's over kadovas broer'

Why what happened? asked Seth.

'Confidential stuff, can't be divulged, but it's a wonder I didn't end up in the Psych ward like your Broer.'

Seth chuckled. 'What a bumma......say how's a light there my china' Champ lean't over to light his slowboat.

All that could be heard from that moment was the slight tapping of feet as Bugsy strummed away, the usual cigarette hanging off the side of his lip, as he screwed up his eyes against the smoke. He and his audience were captivated by the constant cycle of chords which after several strums were repeated and had a hypnotic effect on the drowsy listeners

'Check you later... got business to finish' said the man with the light blue eyes. He arose to his feet and sauntered towards the entrance of the dark cavern. They watched as his silhouette progressively took on colour and light and ascended the ladder.

Suddenly everyone was jolted out of their dream world by a loud thud.

It was the sound of a leather jack boot being slammed into Seth's face, causing him to hurtle back down the ladder landing in a heap at the bottom of the steps. He was not too injured to hollow at the top of his voice. 'Fuzz!'

At that moment, and in one foul swoop, Champ grabbed all the drugs and regalia.

It was as if he had practiced the drill before, and with a swift leap, scrambled up the wall towards the light and somehow squeezed through the tiny slit in the top of the wall, which led out onto the road above and there, he escaped.

Blue uniformed men stalked towards the huddle of youngsters. They were on a mission and that was to flex their legal muscles and arrest and charge all juveniles no matter what their race, who didn't adhere to their strict and very often, obsolete laws.

Handled roughly, the lads were pinned up against the wall, as the drug squad searched each one, breathing threats as they did it. After the ordeal Bugsy picked up his guitar, dusted it off, retrieved his plectrum from the inside of the guitar, and continued on with his constant strumming. It was as if it was his duty to keep alarm at bay and everyone calm, as the proverbial Titanic sank. His three bar chords serenaded them all the way to the station as they sat in the back of the van in which they had been roughly thrown. The strumming faded into the distance eventually, as June was finally escorted home, in a police van, to face her parents.

'Please, please don't take me home', begged June, she tried to get eye contact from her blue uniformed driver. His weather beaten face looked straight ahead at the road.

'Please sir, don't take me home' she said again but this time, she was at the point of bursting into tears. Finally, the policeman showed signs that he was aware of June's desperation and drove straight past her home. Instead, he took her on a tour of the sleezy parts of Durban.

Graveyards, strip clubs, hospitals and pubs, all these were barraged and an endless train of homeless people, addicts and prostitutes were arrested for crimes ranging from vagrancy to possession of drugs.

She could not help but think of the irony of it all. Having started the day with her friends doing illegal things, she had somehow along the line, winded up on the other side of the spectrum. This time on the side of the law accompanying a very cross policeman about his daily tasks.

Finally her driver dropped her at home and told her to 'foetzak!' She peaked cautiously out of the van window first, to check that her mother wasn't doing her daily scanning of the landscape below. When she was assured that the coast was clear, she did a quick translation of the of the busy cop's command.... jumped promptly out of the van and 'beat it!'

CHAPTER 16

*'Don't you ever ask them why, if they told you, you
would cry,
So just look at them and sigh and know they love you. '
Cosby, Stills, Nash and Young 1969*

It was a few days later that June sauntered into her
mother's small, dark room and found her on her knees
in prayer. At being discovered in this odd activity, the
lady got to her feet, straightened her slacks and headed
for the kitchen. June had noticed, that recently she had
been attending the parish church on a regular basis,
hence the new routine of withdrawing into a solitary
place to pray. It was obvious that the couple from the
coffee bar had succeeded at last, to convince mother to
come along to the services. Their continue chipping
away had worked, or perhaps it was their deep concern
that was demonstrated at the death of the little girl that
had turned mother's head in their direction. Anyway
whatever it was, mother was becoming progressively
more religious and June was not sure, quite what to do
about it. The girl followed her to the kitchen, hoping
that there was enough bread to make a sandwich, a little
puzzled at the change of mood in the home.

'You kids should be wearing helmets, you know.
You could have an accident, and then what?' Mother
probed June with the question hoping that it would
strike a chord.

'Oh mum, we can't wear helmits. How ugly is
that!' came the retort. June grabbed her sandwich and
out the door she rushed.

The *Strawberry fields* arrived that evening and so, to celebrate the new cargo, they decided to take a ride to the cane fields where they could experience their *trip* in a new environment. June was not offered any LSD, and kept quiet about the fact that she would be the only one not *high*. It was her conscience that always got in the way of her truly bonding with her friends in this fashion. Finding her mother on her knees in prayer was enough to put her off the thought of disappointing her in that way. She would just have to be an observer, on the outside looking in and that would suffice.

It was raining lightly as they drove past the African, trades women sleeping on the beach, under flimsy plastic shelters that they had rigged up. They were waiting for dawn so that they could display their bead work and carvings to the tourists that drifted past daily.

Down town they continued to drive, past what looked like bundles of rags on the pavements, but in reality, wrapped in the rags were hundreds of poor, homeless black people seeking shelter and a place to sleep under the light of the street lamps. Each one, surely, praying that tomorrow there would be work for them. On they rode past crowds of Africans who were cheering as their favourite boxers fought in the outdoor rings.

The cool raindrops splashed against June's face as she snuggled up close to Henry on his 175cc. They, at last hit the freeway which looked like a long, silver river ahead of them, due to the glimmering moisture which covered the strip of road.

Gary was whooping ecstatically. Imagining himself to be flying, he stretched his arms out against the wind and allowed the long white tassles from his open jacket to flow like angelic wings.

It was Champ who as usual took the lead and was cruising along without a care in the world. Gradually, the silver river, turned rainbow coloured and within seconds, Champ's bike swirled and disappeared off the road. Nobody knew just what had happened. It had been so sudden. The bikers pulled up quickly to the side of the busy freeway and in trepidation, scrambled off their bikes.

The prospects of Champ's body been broken and battered was high. His friends held their breath and clambered down the hill to find him. There was an unnerving silence and the only movement that could be seen was the bike's back wheel which was still spinning. They ran over to find the injured man, who looked curiously smaller as the foetal position which he had landed in, added to the picture of helplessness that was portrayed .

"Champ! My buddy!" cried Henry as he cradled his helmetless head in his arms.

To every one's surprise, at the sound of his name, the big man stirred and opened his eyes, then sat up and shook the debris out of his thick mat of red hair. Looking around at all his concerned friends, shrouded by the light of a far away lamp, he smiled weakly.

his friends helped him to his feet and although he was traumatised, it was noted that he was miraculously unhurt, but his bike was a write off.

***

The experience of that night left June feeling pensive. It had been a close shave for her friend. She marvelled at the fact that he came out of that ordeal with hardly a scratch on him. Yet because of a little bit of oil on a moist surface he could have lost his life.

'I guess it wasn't his time to die' she reflected. 'Perhaps someone was praying for him' came the next thought. Then she remembered her mother on her knees in prayer. The motor bike issue must have been at the top of her prayer list that day, in fact, June was sure that was what her mother must've been praying about.

It was more than coincidental, that Sue decided to pay June a visit a little while after the episode. They sat on the bed together and chatted about this and that.

'How are you getting on with your Christian walk?' asked Sue, in a matter of fact way. June put her hand on her chin and looked into the air thoughtfully.

'frankly, I think I'm doing ok' she answered proudly. 'You know my friends take drugs, but I'm adamant that I won't go down that road.'

She sat up straight and put out her chest proudly and vocalised her thoughts by saying, 'I think I'm quite good really. Mmm.'

Finding herself in a contemplative mood, she then continued,

'I am becoming a bit more aware that Jesus is walking with me...and with my friends' Her confidence was mounting, so she launched into a descriptive account of Champ's brush with death.

'That's wonderful! How amazing that he was not hurt at all!' answered Susan whose face lit up in genuine amazement, but within seconds the radiance disappeared and was replaced by a serious expression.

'but I feel I must leave you with these words from the Bible, June. [xxvii]*"Take heed when ye think ye stand, lest ye fall"*

Her smile disappeared and she held June's attention by looking deep into her eyes. Such contact was intense enough to cause June to feel a tinge of annoyance that Sue wasn't congratulating her on her success of abstinence from the vices that her friends were using. She wasn't saying the things that June wanted to hear and June was incensed at that.

'Typical!' Thought June as she waved goodbye to Sue from the balcony. 'Christians they're so hard to please!'

CHAPTER 17

In a white room with black curtains. Cream 1966

June had found a simpler form of transport in the form of a 'chopper bicycle. This had resolved the problem of having to hustle a lift off guys that June hardly knew. She had learned the hard way, when, one day, having nothing to do, she had consented to go for a ride with a biker who she hardly knew and ended up in the cane fields all alone with a big man who looked more like a heavy weight boxer than a peace loving surfer. Things could have gone awfully wrong for June, if he had not decided to take her home when she said 'stop'.

Then she had tried to become more ambitious by trying to chat up a national surfing champion named Robbie. For two reasons this attempt was made. One because he was a man with a van, a VW 1969 Combie, which could be used for her advantage that's if she played her cards right and won his attention. This would be a plus for her, seeing he was good looking and had social standing. To expand on the idea it would definitely have shifted her into another league....a sort of career move, if you please. With quick precision though, he made it clear to her in no uncertain terms that she was totally out of his league. So that was the end of that idea.

Curiously, she observed the state of another combie van, which was filled with all the regalia of a surfing crowd, that is surfboards, surfers and bikini girls. They whizzed up and down the beachfront daily. Surely there would be room for one more she reasoned. Yet, after reflecting on the state of the vehicle, which was rapidly deteriorating and losing significant parts, like the doors for example, she decided against it, especially since the young 'cowboy' at the wheel went around corners at 45 degree angles, almost certain to dispose of the poor passengers who were already hazardously exposed to the elements because of the absence of the doors. Even though the problem was lackadaisically solved by the insertion of a plank of wood to keep all and sundry contained, June thought it not worth the effort to put herself out there to become part of the circle. No, a bicycle would suffice. It was safer that way, in more ways than one, especially since the back of the combie was easily converted into a bed, if luck was on the side of the owner.

This novelty of getting around independently, meant that she could travel in peace as she glided along the beach front, enjoying her new found freedom . A trip from the South beach to the North beach took no time at all and the expansion of space also meant a potential increase in her social interaction with those on the other side of her little world, namely the North Beach. It became routine to wave at all her new found friends, as she rode swiftly past.

On this particular day, she jumped off her bicycle at the back of the XL cafe, because she spotted her friend Barbara. The girl had changed a lot over the years and now hung out with the 'Alley Cats'. These were chain and flick knife wielding individuals who decorated themselves with tattoos and their personal hygiene had a lot to be desired, seeing that washing was not on top of their priority list. Barbara had taken on the veneer all too easily and was, at that present time, drinking far too much, observed June.

Although these [xxviii]*duck tails* were not too friendly with the likes of June, whose appearance and speech presented her to be far too English for their liking, they tolerated her, because of her long time friendship with one of their favourite *cherries*.

The pleasant aroma of hamburgers wafted in the air and added to the attraction of joining her long time friend on the pavement, at the back of the Cafe'. She flopped down next to Barbara who was sitting in the shade, looking in the opposite direction from the sand and surf. This group did everything opposite to the regular surfing crowd.

The surfers smoked weed and spoke of peace and making love and spent their holidays at Jeffrey's Bay and got around on dirt bikes or scramblers. While the Alley Cats, drank hard liquor and practiced violence and spent their spare time in prison and had an affinity for very large, fast, road bikes.

The Alley Cats hated the surfer dudes and the surfers were scared of the Alley Cats. All these insights made June reflect philosophically about her mission between the two groups. She had started to think deeply about many things lately, thanks to Mr Scott's thought provoking literature lessons.

Barbara's new tattoo was still fresh and scabby. It read *Billy the Kid*. Which June gathered was her new boyfriend.

'You mean to say you've never heard of the Billy the Kid? scolded Barbara, when June revealed her ignorance of his person.

'He's the most well know [xxix]*jawler* in Jo Burg' continued Barbara with pride, and dropped her shoulders slightly, as she added.

[xxx]'Yuh, but he's in the *clink,* cos he *dondered* a *rooinek* outside of the *Cockney Pride*.' *Rooinek* was slang for English man and June was a bit puzzled that she had adopted the term, since Barbara, herself, was one of those hated *rooineks*. It seemed like she had left

her roots altogether to join the Boer's cause, as if the Boer war was still raging.

That was it! A light was suddenly switched on in her head!

Was it not she, who was to be the peace maker between the Boers and the English? Or the *mods* and the *rockers,* the *Hippie* surfers and the *Ducktails...* whatever! She finally had a purpose for her existence and it was all down to the presence of her bicycle, which helped her to cover the miles between the two camps.

It seemed though, that she was not the only one commuting between the two camps for, from around the corner, eloped a lone surfer boy, dripping from head to foot. He left wet puddles on the tarmac, as he approached the group of leather clad bikers. Still panting from his workout in the surf, he lean't his board up against the brick wall and launched into a discussion with one of the Alley Cats. June couldn't help noticing his slim physique and felt strangely drawn to him. She made up her mind that she was going to get to know this guy a little better. He definitely didn't fit the Alley cat mould. He, without question was in the hippy camp. Not that his hair was long or anything, in fact it was short and spiky, and emphasized his pointed, pixie like ears. June withdrew herself a little more into the shade so that she could study him more closely without him noticing her. She observed that he had fine features and long graceful fingers. She guessed that he was a musician, perhaps a pianist or something. She also hoped that he wouldn't notice her, hanging out with the *Duck Tails..* She would hate him to think that she was one of *them...* but too late, he had already glanced her way and taken note of her sitting there.

After the business proposition, they exchanged a secret hand shake and without further ado, he turned on his heels in her direction and sauntered towards her. His lips creased into a crooked smile which was meant only for her, and with confident assertiveness, he invited June to accompany him to Tim's place.

Tim was a legend. He had surfed for South Africa and had won international status. June only knew about him, but had never had the opportunity to mix in circles where he hung out. Now was her chance. Without even a second thought, she was by his side and looked back only to say goodbye to her friend.

The two of them weaved their way through the back streets of Durban away from the tall hotels that were so enjoyed by the tourists. There was no conversation between them, but this didn't bother June. It seemed like they had a connection which was beyond words and speech did not seem to be necessary.

Up a damp, dark stair case, they ascended and entered an apartment, very much like the ones that June was frequenting as of late. A formidable figure sat in the middle of the floor with trimmings of leather all around him and a heap of marijuana piled up beside him on some newspaper. June guessed that this was the well known surfer in person. Everyone around him was in a jubilant mood. He was celebrating his five hundredth trip on LSD (so he said) and his circle of animated friends were congratulating him and hoping that there would be a cocktail of drugs on the house for the evening.

June felt suddenly shy and looked up at her tall escort, who had already moved away from her, when somebody called 'Hey Jimmy!'

She stood awkwardly for a moment and noticed Tim's intense stare, it made her feel uncomfortable and she deliberately moved away from his line of vision. She was relieved to see Kenny in the corner sitting on a bean bag. He hadn't been down to the South beach for a long time and now she knew why. To her surprise, he was still small in stature and 'little Kenny' continued to be an apt name for him. He seemed quite at home in his surroundings and appeared to be enjoying the abundance of drugs which were available to him. June tried to look casual and sidled up to him. In her awkwardness she attempted to chat to him, by asking him where he was staying?

'Here' was the brief answer.

She continued to try to strike up conversation.

'How is Isabelle?' she asked,

genuinely interested in the whereabouts of his sister.

There was eye contact, but for a moment and he answered as briefly as possible

'I think she's in the Cape with Mick'

He lowered his big green eyes making it obvious that he didn't want to talk any more, especially if it was going to be an interrogation of a hundred and one questions. He went back to patiently waiting for the next pipe to be lit and passed around.

It was all so depressing, and June was beginning to feel increasingly out on a limb, until someone announced from the balcony that the Alley Cats were hurling abusive threats at them.

The chain and flick knife wielding opposition had moved to an apartment across the road and the unfortunate had happened. ...the Hippies and the Alley Cats had become neighbours! Suddenly everyone in the room formed a united front against the common enemy and June was immediately accepted into the circle and swept up in the wave of comradeship. A sense of belonging overwhelmed her, even if it was just to make up the numbers against the enemy. She forgot that only half an hour ago, she was hiding in the shadows with the Alley Cats and Jimmy had been too. Nevertheless, this unfolding of events didn't seem to bother Jimmy in any way, after all he was their go between. They would not harm him because that would cut off their drug supply. With confidence in that knowledge, he ventured out to get a much needed carton of milk from the corner store, so that the tea would continue to flow once more.

He returned in good time, the way that Tim had already predicted, with blood pouring down his face and a great gash in his head. It was obvious that the Alley Cats would not tolerate any exceptions in this war against the hippies. Jimmy was simply one of them, so, he deserved a hole in the head.

This was a perfect chance for June to be alone with him and she seized the opportunity by leading him to the bathroom to nurse his wound, that actually, appeared worse than what it really was. Now was June's chance to use all her wily charms on her patient and she bent over him to reveal her well stocked bra. At this invitation, he nestled his face in the cleft of her bosom and marvelled at the turn of events and the luck that he had landed in .....a soft landing at that!

CHAPTER 18

To see the World in a Grain of Sand
And Heaven in a Wild Flower,
Hold Infinity in the palm of your hand
And Eternity in an hour   William Blake

It was the next day that things started to unfold that made June think she had lost control. It all happened so fast. One moment she was walking along with her new boyfriend and the next moment, found her in the backseat of a fast moving car with a group of excited people going up the coast to a deserted beach. Minutes before, she had swallowed a quarter cap of LSD, because her new boyfriend had told her to do so. How could she say no? She just couldn't. She was just sixteen and he was in his twenties, he was sure to know best. After all she just wanted to be with him, and this was the best way to really connect with him.

After a quick stop off at the phone booth to let her mother know that she would be home late, June's anxiety lessened. Her mother worried if she didn't hear from June and spent many a sleepless night waiting for her to come home. It was all such a burden, ruminated the girl, as she closed her eyes to try and erase the sadness on her mother's face if she got wind of what her daughter was up to.

The landscape became increasingly tropical as it sped by. Every imaginable fruit tree came and went from view until the cloudless sky met the sea with a kiss from a seamless horizon. It was a perfect day she told herself. This was something that she had planned to do.

Even in art class the students discussed the benefits of turning on to hallucinogens, because it helped to trigger the imagination and so enhanced the ideas that were expressed on the canvas, so she was told.

Then, of course there was [xxxi]Timothy Leary, whose books on the benefits of being *turned on*, had been recommended to her and she had been an avid reader of such literature for a good few months.

It was only a matter of time, she told herself, that this moment would come.

She remembered how Foxy accommodated his unconventional, drug orientated views by taking some arbitrary scripture from the [xxxii]Book of Revelation. It was when Jesus was giving his disciples advice about anointing their eyes with eye salve. In Foxy's befuddled state of mind, this was an instruction to participate in the hallucinogenic experience. He did not stop to think that he was doing what every cultist does....taking verses out of context ....but then, she reasoned that the whole book of Revelation was like a hallucination, so perhaps he had a point.

Clutching Jimmy's hand, nervously, she waited for the experience to begin. The sky appeared bluer than usual . A flock of birds flew across the sky and she had the sensation of flying with them.

Eventually when they reached their destination, the excited youngsters burst from the confines of the car to discover a rocky beach. The rock formation had already taken on a life of its own. In fact everything seemed alive and animated.

A man with an enormous, tawny coloured dog on a lead sauntered past. Its every bristle of fur appeared to be living and trying to make contact with the awe struck girl.

June held Jimmy's hand for awhile but soon found that she needed to be on her own, connecting, in a mystical way, with the world which appeared to be embracing her with great joy. She felt like a tiny microcosm perched on the chest of a giant, trembling creature, bathed in crystal colours, like a mother rocking its child into an ecstatic, illusive state. The sensation of something living and breathing beneath her, and the rhythm of such, created a feeling of enchantment, an aspiring to a higher dimension. Numbers and symbols formed in the white fluffy clouds which had swept across the sky with the north, westerly breeze and suddenly she felt like a genius who could work out all the difficult mathematical equations ever discovered, she felt so grand, a goddesss in the making.

No wonder Jimmy spoke so little. He was beyond all that. He was in direct contact with the universe, she thought, looking up at him, as he sat on the highest pinnacle of the cliff face, above the sea.

Grant it, had she not been warned about guys like him? Was it not a feather in his cap to turn as many girls as possible onto LSD? If she remembered rightly..yes... she had been warned, but the temptation had been too great. There was something about the chemical which caused a person to want to venerate...to find an object or creature to worship. Who better than the one who introduced such an experience! Would it not be that individual who became the focal point for adoration?

She remembered seeing Isabelle on the beach, kneeling at Foxy's feet in complete devotion to him, because he had been the first one to turn her on to LSD. Now she totally understood why Isabelle acted so strangely.

At that moment Jimmy looked like a god. He had given her the gift of this wonderful experience. What could she give him in return? Within hours June's structured life style with its built in value system had crumbled. Her mother had always reminded her that it was easier to say 'no' to the boys than 'yes', and she would be rewarded with the respect which she deserved. June saw the logic in her mother's advice and followed it willingly. But at that moment it was Yes! Yes! Yes! to Jimmy for any favours he may have asked of her. All her inhibitions suddenly dissolved in the cosmic phenomenon.

CHAPTER 19

O Rose thou art sick. The invisible worm,
That flies in the night In the howling storm:
Has found out thy bed of crimson joy:
And his dark secret love does thy life destroy.
Wiliam Blake

No matter how June tried she could not capture on canvas the magic of that day. The surrealism, the depth of colour, the dimensions..all of them were unobtainable and inexpressible. So she grew increasingly dissatisfied with her efforts. Eventually she resorted to deep, dark colours, which she splashed across the canvas, revealing feelings of abandonment and frustration. Big black birds rising out of a menacing dark sea became her favourite subject. Her mother tried to hide her alarm at this new phase in the budding artist's life. It didn't take a psychologist to realize that something slightly sinister had happened to her disturbed daughter.

Frustrated with her numerous attempts to relive that day by painting it, June resorted to writing about it. That was the easier option. At least she would never forget that one experience by recording it on paper. After all, Jimmy had mysteriously disappeared off the face of the earth. He had come and gone. The bewildered teen wandered around the beach looking for him but no one seemed to know where he was. She would have tried to contact him through his parents, but didn't know how to, all that was known was that his dad played the violin in the Durban philharmonic orchestra.

Her heart was sore, where could he be, she wondered? It dawned on her that she was in love but such a transient emotion could not be realized, if the recipient wasn't available. As the days went by the hope of seeing him again, faded.

***

In the meantime, college was endured on a daily basis. The emptiness she felt was unbearable. All motivation had ebbed away from her and her daily objective was to return to her bed as soon as possible.

 By the light of a lamp in her dark room she paged through her pile of books which were becoming increasingly occultic in nature. Her collection was growing rapidly.

To escape from her feelings of depression, she started to explore the practice of astral projection through certain meditation exercises, but these activities only added to her feelings of futility. The lyrics of Jimi Hendrix advertising 'Purple Haze and Jim Morrison advocating the opening of doors to the soul added to her perplexity. John Lennon was prompting her to imagine a new world, where there was no heaven and no religion. There didn't seem much to live for and definitely nothing to die for, so what the heck.... a hedonistic life style was the way to go. Yet she was appalled at the fact that she was not succeeding in that particular pursuit, either.

***

It was Friday night and June was not going to sit at home. Grabbing her jacket, she went to join her friends on the beach. There was a West wind blowing gently

118

and the sun was setting . It was a beautiful evening. The boys on their bikes were pulling in, parking, and settling down on the grass. The animated youngsters were making plans for the next day to go across to the other side of the harbour, by ferry, to the whaling station, where they would spend the day at the old bomb shelters which had been built on the beach, during the 2nd World War. It was always a good day out, with plenty of music, food and other things, and June was used to returning home sun burnt but happy. Now she felt far from happy. She reclined on the grass, and imagined Jimmy by her side. Nobody seemed too interested in her presence, which added to her feeling of abandonment.

Her girlfriends had turned up at beach and had warmly greeted each other with a kiss yet the sensitive soul felt that they had excluded her from their company by deliberately ignoring her. Her underlying insecurities and lack of confidence were perceived from this premise.

Suddenly Seth pulled in on his bike, screeching on brakes he jumped from the saddle and strided towards the motley group lounging around on the grass. He was on a mission and his eyes seemed more piercingly blue than usual. Overwhelmed with excitement, he stood in front of his friends and declared in a loud voice

'Jesus is alive and he loves you all very much!' at that, he rummaged through a grubby packet which he was carrying and presented a pile of New Testaments and began to hand them out one by one. Everyone was surprised, because usually it was LSD or Magic Mushroom that he was marketing to his friends. He launched into a short sermon, got back on his bike again and drove off at full speed leaving a trail of smoke behind him.

Everyone was gob smacked! This was not the Seth that they knew. The Seth they knew was too busy trying to supply everyone with their favourite drug. No one knew exactly what to say or think. It was Bruce the Scotsman who made the first comment.

'Ag the man has a wee bit of religion, he'll be back to normal in a week.'

June took a pull on her cigarette, picked up her jacket and her New Testament and made her way home.

She threw her jacket over her shoulder and entered her apartment, hoping to find her mother in the kitchen making a meal for her, but it wasn't to be. Instead her mother was standing in the narrow corridor. Her face looked stern in the half light and her freshly made up, red lips were pursed and sad . At this point June sensed that there was something terribly wrong, because her mother only used that particular, blood red lipstick when she was upset about something.

The shifty youth did not know what to do, so attempted to squeeze past the human obstruction which was in her way by mumbling politely under her breath. She had never seen her mother in such a confrontational mode and the determined woman stood her ground and would not move.

'What's wrong mum?' she asked curiously. There was a moment of silence, as her mother thought about what to say.

'I know what you've been up to' came the stilted reply. June let out a nervous giggle.

'what do you mean?' she answered, trying to stay calm by keeping a weak smile on her face.

'Your diary, it fell out of the cupboard, while I was tidying up, and this is the page it fell on...I, I couldn't help but read it.' Mother's voice began to break and her hand trembled as she presented the little book to her daughter.

'Why are you taking drugs? Why.....?' tears welled up in her eyes.

'Mum it won't happen again, don't worry. It was only one time. Please don't worry!' she exclaimed, doing her best to console the distraught woman.

Unexpectedly, her mother took a deep breath, and with surprising boldness, exclaimed,

'I will not let the devil get you. Do you hear me...He's not having you!'

She handed the diary back to her daughter and withdrew to her bedroom.

June looked at her diary, her experience with Jimmy had been recorded in colourful detail. She sat down on the end of the bed and gazed down at the diary and the little New Testament next to it. She did not feel annoyed that the inquisitive woman was rummaging around in her cupboard in the first place, only the feeling of sadness lingered.

***

Bruce was right, It only took one week for Seth to revert back to his old self. What Bruce didn't know, though, was that *he* would be the target for Seth's temporary insanity while he was high on LSD. It was a bloody night, as Seth whipped around the room in a violent frenzy, attacking everyone in his view.

Unfortunately Bruce got within striking distance and received a couple of vicious blows which landed him with a bloody nose and cut lip. Somehow or other June crossed Seth's path and was dragged down the corridor by her hair.

She desperately tried to keep her cool and managed to calm him down and get him out of his terrified frame of mind. She was afraid that he might throw himself down the stairs like one of the lads had done a few weeks before and took some serious injuries in the process and was then carted off to hospital by his mother who was a psychiatric nurse.

The young revellers were shaken up when eventually the nightmare party ended. In Bruce's mind, though, the nightmare had not ended. He was not going to let Seth off the hook that easily, so he continued to torment him, by flashing his bloody countenance in the terrified man's face for the rest of the evening, determined to make him more miserable than ever. The evening had taken a bizarre turn for the worst and although it was comical in a dark sort of way, June could only sum it up as just plain frightening, as she made her way home on her own.

She felt that her friends were all going mad. Seth had been like a wild animal. His brother, Luke was still in hospital and several of her friends seemed to be following in his footsteps.

It was becoming common to hear that one of her company had winded up in that ominous institution on the hill and was undergoing treatment by the staff in white whose main solution was to whip the non complaint patients onto numbing medication after a series of [xxxiii]'shock treatment'. Where would it all end and how could she escape from such a life?

CHAPTER 20

'Come on all of you big strong men
Uncle Sam needs a helping hand
Got himself in a terrible jam'
Country Joe and the Fish 1969

'Let me in June, I need a favour' It was Bobby at the door. He was carrying a large kit bag over his shoulder and was looking more anxious than ever. June held the door opened for him and he quickly stumbled inside .

'Please, I need a place to store my army kit!' came the urgent request.

'Sure', June shrugged her shoulders it was no big deal. 'What was the problem, why was he so uptight?' she thought.

Bobby ambled quickly into June's room,

'The MP's are after me' he continued under his breath as he threw his heavy kit onto the already cluttered bed.

Before June could ask 'why?' he was already answering.

'Because I've awolled.'

June was not too perturbed that Bobby had run away from the army and now the Military Police were after him, this was a common activity among the Durban army boys, who were mainly of English descent, and begrudgingly gave up to two years of their lives to uphold the apartheid policy.

Mr Scott had said that the Apartheid was born on the back of the dying embers of facism which was brought over from Germany after the second world war. It made sense that most of the boys found it difficult to uphold such a policy, this she was well aware of, especially since Durban was known as the 'last British outpost'. On the other hand, she was blissfully ignorant of the implications of Bobby, getting caught , until he continued.

'If they catch me, I'll be going to prison again.... the last time they made me eat pencils!' He said, stumbling over his words.

'pencils?' June was amused at such a thing.

'Yes, pencils, they made me eat led! I can't go back there! They're on my trail, right now as we speak!'

She held the cupboard door opened so that he could cram all his army clothes onto the top shelf.

At that moment there was a knock at the door. Bobby looked with alarm at June, who at last had realized the urgency of the moment.

'Get into the cupboard' she said excitedly pushing the clothes aside so that he could crouch in the corner. She spread the clothes out around him and closed the door. Marching towards the front door, she thought for a moment what she would say to the military police to get them off Bobby's trail. She took a deep breath and with boldness, opened the door. Her eyes instinctively looked upwards at nothing...then down at her little friend, Rachel, who stood forlornly on the threshold wiping her eyes with a tissue.

Like a little torpedo, Rachel pushed passed her hostess and aimed straight for the bedroom. With anguished cries, she threw herself over the only spot on the bed that wasn't covered with non essential items and began to wail at the top of her voice. June ran to the bathroom to get a roll of tissue paper, this was going to be a long night.

While Rachel buried her head in the pillow, June opened the cupboard door and released Bobby, who ran

124

out the front door and down the road to find refuge somewhere else.

'I hate him!...how could he do such a thing to me..' she stammered.

June had no idea what Rachel was talking about. Who was this person that she hated? It couldn't possibly be a boyfriend. She had no idea that Rachel had one special boy in her life.

'He slept with me and then went straight out and slept with ....Charmaine!' at the name 'Charmaine'

Rachel began to wail even louder and unrolled a wad of tissue paper. June got the rubbish bin and placed it within throwing distance for Rachel.

'Who? Who are you talking about?'

'Shane, I thought he loved me.....but then he went straight out and slept with Charmaine'

She was battling to catch her breath and took another wad of tissue paper. June was aware that the toilet roll was rapidly depleting.

'You mean Tim's mate, Shane? Rachel why didn't you tell me?'

Her exasperated voice had an edginess about it, like that of a parent chiding a child.

'Charmaine.... of all people. She's so slutty... and yet he brazenly went straight to her, after being with me........that's what I meant to him....nothing!...nothing!.' she wailed unconsolably.

June's friend was truly heartbroken. Gently, yet feeling a little lost for words, she leant over to comfort the smaller girl who was by this time in a foetal position on the bed. To stroke her hair and hand her the last piece of tissue from the roll, was all she could do. There was nothing else which could wipe the pain away...the damage had been done.

Rachel had given this young, handsome heart breaker her virginity and he had gone out and made a statement that her love meant nothing to him.

'So these are the goings on at Tim's place, no wonder he looked at me so intently' reflected June, as she continued to comfort her friend. It all made sense now, the way the guys casually, filtered out of Tim's flat one by one, when Jimmy arrived with June on his arm, after that memorable day at the beach. It was obvious that they were all hoping that Jimmy would 'get lucky' with her in bed, being routine amongst the lads. Instead, Jimmy's attention was turned to the bongo drums in the corner of the room at June's bidding, and the evening was spent in a drum circle duet, which ended up with the neighbours complaining about the noise.

'Pretty nerdie huh?' reflected June.

She remembered that Tim's chat up line had been quite cheesy really, but possibly from the lips of someone else, could have had an effect. The line was, that she reminded him of a juicy peach ready for taking a bit out of. Of course, this metaphor coming from the wizened old surfer, had an adverse effect on June and only made her more adamant that he wasn't getting any of her!

But returning to the issue at hand, here was her poor friend whose little frame was convulsing with grief. She had been betrayed and deceived by one of Tim's young mates. What cads they all were!

She patted and stroked Rachel gently, rubbing her back, until the convulsing stopped and there was a period of calm. It was then that she thought of her own pain. Yes, she knew, to some degree what it was to be used, abused and abandoned. Had not Jimmy done that to her, by coming into her life and turning her on to something that she could not turn off....a hunger to see him again? Plus, he had robbed her of enjoying her life, for nothing could compare to that fabulous day, every other day was dim and dull in the light of it.

Where was he? That's what she'd like to know!

After Rachel had been bundled into a taxi and sent home, June wearily got into her pyjamas, breathing a sigh of relief that her parents had spent the day out during all the dramas that had ensued. She was just about to go to bed when there was another knock at the door.

'Who is it?' she asked before opening the door.

' Military Police here, we would like to speak to you please, Miss Paine.'

CHAPTER 21

'All I want is the truth, just give me the truth!'
John Lennon (Imagine)1971

Besides the Military Police and their task to catch up with the deserters, there was the South African Police who had formed a specialized force called the 'Drug Squad' to track down the drug smugglers and their merchants who sold the drugs on the streets.

She and her friends, had already experienced a run in with the drug squad and June was not prepared to experience their brutality again, but on this occasion a new tactic was used to infiltrate the drug culture.

It all began one evening, when a young man approached June, claiming that he was from Kenya. This bit of information was enough common ground to trigger a friendship and it did not take long for him to ask her out on a date. Perhaps this was destined to be her means of escape from the drug underworld which was beginning to pull her progressively down. The gradual descent could be alluded to the strong and sporadic currents of the sea, which often put the unsuspecting bather into a place of deadly danger.

Anyway, hopes were raised at the pleasant turn of events and her parents delight at the prospect of a decent young man coming into their daughter's life could not be hidden. He, without doubt, did not fit in with the surfing culture and it conjured up memories for June of her early introduction to such a company of young people. She could empathise and determined to be kind to him. He appeared to be such a respectable chap from her childhood home she thought.

On the night of the date, her parents showed their approval by giving little comments like

'your hair looks so beautiful Darling.... Oh you do look especially nice tonight dear.... Don't forget to wear the earrings I bought you for your birthday ....'

and on and on it went. Her mother tended at times like this to live her life through her daughter. It was as if *she* was going out on the date.

When he arrived, the delighted matriarch fussed over him and chatted about Kenya, she was not put off when he kept changing the subject, and he sighed with relief when June announced that she was ready to go.

It was when they got into the car, that he let her know that they were going to a party. June was a bit disappointed as she was under the impression that he had invited her out for a meal, but she shrugged it off and did not let it worry her.

It was only when they got to the party that she started to have suspicions about the young man's true identity.

'I have some really potent tabs with me tonight' He whispered, as they stood out on the balcony of the large apartment.

'I have a cocktail here, purple hearts, red devils, black bombs....we can have a real rave! ' He gave a wicked little chuckle and held her gaze. June shook her head and smiled weakly. She looked around at the revellers and felt very much out of place. Their demeanor and appearance seemed strange to her.

She couldn't help but notice how athletic and regimental the women looked, with their short, cropped hair. Like peas in a pod. It seemed as if they had all emerged from the same pod.

They all had a certain look about them that June couldn't quite figure out. Sitting there, together laughing, downing bottles of liquor, they made her think of people who played hard and worked hard. She wondered where they hung out, definitely not on the beach front. She asked one of them what they did, but the woman just laughed and went to mingle somewhere else. Her date brought over a bottle of whisky and offered June a glass, but June felt too uncomfortable. She wasn't a drinker. Drink made her melancholy. Fair enough, if he was prepared to sit in a corner with her and her bottle, while she rambled on between sobs about her rubbish life but somehow, she didn't feel that this was his objective for getting her drunk. She felt it was a little more complicated than that. He had offered her tabs and now he was trying to get her to drink hard liquor. What was the motive here, she wondered?

Much to June's relief, he suggested a slow drive home. It turned out to be a very slow drive.

'So tell me about your friends?' he said casually.

'What would you like to know?' answered June, as she gazed vacantly out the window, thinking how glad she was that the night had been prematurely terminated.

'What do they like to do?'

'Oh this and that, surfing mainly.' She yawned.

'Do they turn on?' He asked awkwardly, as if the phrase was new to his vocabulary.

She looked at him thoughtfully and wondered why he was asking such a direct question. The weary side of her, needed a shoulder to cry on, somebody who she could confide in but the wary side of her felt a check . The weary side won out.

'Ummm sometimes, and then they all end up in hospital'.

'Really?'

'Yeh, like, last week Seth had to coax one of our friends down from the 14th floor of the building because he was going to jump. He thought he could fly, you know.' It was as if June was thinking out loud as she rambled on.

'Oh yeh? That must've have been quite frightening. This Seth does he have a 175 Yamaha?'

'Yes.' She said absently.

'What's his surname and where does he live?' Alarm bells went off suddenly, in June's head.

'Why do you want to know all this?' with June, it always took awhile for the penny to drop but at last it had. As well as that, she was incensed that he was not showing an interest in her.

Her date drove the car into a parking space outside her home. Reached under the seat and for dramatic effect, pulled out a police baton, declaring,

'because I am a cop that works for the drug squad.... and everything you have said has been recorded right here.' He opened the cubby hole to reveal a hidden tape recorder.

June looked at him in amazement. Astonished and angry, she clambered quickly out of the car. Slammed the door in disgust and rushed into the building.

Mum and Dad wondered why she was back so early but she was in no mood to share her experience with them. Throwing down her bag, she quickly made her way to her bedroom and closed the door behind her. The last thing she wanted to do was draw attention to herself. She pondered on what to say to her parents. There was no way she could tell them the truth that her date had tried to use her as a pawn to inform on the movements of her friends. This would have been to admit that, not just some of her friends but *all* her friends were part of the drug culture. Letting them in to the reality of her life would be a mistake, she resolved as she held back the tears and regained her composure. She sauntered back to the lounge and perched herself uncomfortably on a chair bracing herself for the interrogation.

'Fire away' she thought, looking at her parents expectant faces, as the questions began.

Skillfully, untruth after untruth proceeded from her smiling lips as she weaved a perfect tale, which put her parents at peace about the evening.

At last, she returned to her room and lay in the dark. The night was still. Mum and Dad had gone to bed. In her reclined position, she recalled everything that had been said to the policeman and hoped that her clumsy conversation had not incriminated her friends. She wondered what the police did with all the drugs that they took off people, because her date seemed to have access to a copious amount of amphetomines. It must've been a temptation for them to experiment with the evidence perhaps even more so than the kids on the streets.

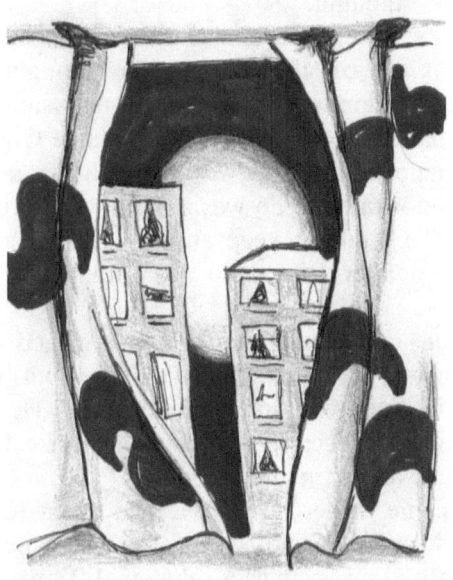

The moon was peaking through the buildings. Its mellow light caressed her face. Oh how soothing the moon was! Not like the invasive harshness of the sun. She could look straight into the face of the moon and not have to squint. Its light did not interrogate her, but wooed her lovingly. She loved the night more than the day. Nothing was expected of her at night. That's when the world unwound from the tight knot that the day created. It was at night that she could be herself, without having to perform for anyone. She didn't have to lie anymore or be somebody else. The masks could be removed, because the darkness hid her true self anyway. Like a tape recorder in her mind she went over everything that had been said. The *feds* were obviously watching Seth. The least she could do was warn him. She looked up at the moon and prayed. Maybe there was a moon goddess, who she could to talk to, who wouldn't judge her or expect anything from her, she thought.

If there was a goddess, she was sure to be gentler than the God of the bible. Her thoughts were unravelling randomly and in quick succession, taking on a spiritual element. She began to blame God for all that was happening. Life wasn't much fun anymore. All that God wanted to do was shackle her to rules and laws that she couldn't keep anyway. There must be something gentler out there...it would have to be feminine.

For some odd reason, her thoughts turned towards Jesus. He was a man....that was true...but he was definitely in touch with his feminine side. He seemed to symbolize the decade. The whole 'make love not war' notion was summed up in Him.

Dave, came to her mind. He had taken too much magic mushroom and now he had grown a beard and insisted on gliding around in robes with flowers in his long flowing hair, because he was convinced that he was Jesus.

Then there was the long playing record called *Jesus Christ Superstar*, which Bugsy had offered her because he was going to throw it out, anyway. She had grown accustomed to the lyrics, and discovered the music that no-one wanted had become a bit of a treasure to her. Two ideas seemed to sum up how she viewed Jesus. He was a kind of self sacrificing Hippy whose mission went wrong, somehow.

She pondered over the Eastern philosophy that Liam, a new comer to her group of friends, was promoting. No-one seemed very interested in what he had to say, but June had showed an interest. It seemed like a door into her soul had been opened up and she could not close it. Eastern mysticism suddenly seemed so attractive. It was all those goddesses that she could get in contact with, she reasoned...Yes ..Hinduism with all its gods was the route to take, she decided..

Her eyes followed the silvery light into the midnight sky, which ended in a knot around a cloud covering the moon. Her lovely moon was veiled, it was time to sleep to take her mind off the unpleasant events of the night and dream of female deities.... and of course, Jimmy, but where oh where was Jimmy?

CHAPTER 22

Black Magic Woman
Got your spell on me Baby.
Don't turn your back on me Baby
Santana 'Abraxas'1969

It turned out that Liam was born under the same astrological star as Rachel. They were both Cancerians. June's theory was that she was compatible with Cancerians, even though they were water signs and she was a fire sign. A mystery, she could not quite understand. Her attitude of astrological discrimination had developed through her interaction with people. If she was not compatible with them, she would blame it on their particular star sign, thus, everyone born in that month would be painted with the same brush and subsequently avoided.

Liam was therefore, in her good books and an agreeable working relationship could commence. June now had her own spiritual guide.

Unfortunately, there was one problem that hindered June's journey to spiritual enlightenment and that was Liam's persistent fear of his wife's reaction to the knowledge that he had a rather delectable devotee.

Liam's wife was a witch.

So, while he trudged the peaceful, meditative path to enlightenment and eventual nirvana with his small group of devotees, his wife was exercising her occultist muscles through ritual and spells.

He spent his time and effort detaching himself from his ego and she spent her time strengthening her ego through the manipulation of the powers of nature.

He was trying to become one with the universe and she was busy trying to control the universe.

He was talking to his avatars and she was presumably getting possessed by her spirit guides.

June could not help but think that it was all going to end in disaster, so, she kept her nose steadfastly in the books that he recommended and obediently followed his example during the meditation sessions. Although she found the philosophy just about as tangled up and confusing as the many deities that she was introduced to, she pressed on like a good devotee should.

Finally it all came to a head one day, when Liam was knocked down by a car as he was crossing the road to his house. From then on, it was impossible, because of his plastered leg, for him get into the lotus position. Hence, the mystical quality of the meditation session was irreparably damaged, due to Liam's sporadic yelps of pain at crucial moments when his devotees were drifting blissfully into the lower plains of Nirvana.

'I'm really sorry about all this' sighed Liam, as he laid his crutches on the floor, hoping that he would not have to commence a meditation session with June, who was secretly relieved, as she couldn't bear to see him in such pain when trying to contort his body into yoga positions. There was a sense that he needed to talk anyway, she perceived.

He struggled to sit down on a chair, positioning his leg so that it didn't cause an obstruction.

'What exactly happened?' asked June.

'Do you really want me to be frank with you?'

June nodded. She looked curiously under her brow up at him from the floor where she was sitting on a cushion.

'Well, I reckon it's my wife that caused this.'

June's expression must have given her away, as she looked doubtfully at him.

No, No...this is not a "my wife doesn't understand me line"...honestly.' He interjected defensively,

'She has these powers you see. She says she's a white witch, but really she's not, because when angry, she's as black as black can be....do you know what I mean?..well she's been mad with me lately....I'm spending too much time with my devotees. The silly woman's very jealous and doesn't like me hanging out with certain ones.'

He looked at June sideways and continued,

'so I guess this is my punishment.' He said resignedly and pointed to his leg.

June was puzzled.

'Are you saying that you think that your wife caused the accident?' She asked. There was a hint of unbelief in her tone of voice.

'I do' he answered decisively without a moment's hesitation.

'That car came from nowhere. It was a hit and run, the guy just went right on driving'.

He looked down at June and held her gaze. The puzzled youth, didn't quite know how to respond to his convictions. She suddenly remembered the game of [xxxiv]glassy- glassy which she played with her friends. Yes, that day there were definitely spirits twirling the glass around. Whether they were good or bad, she could not tell but the spirit world was real, that, she was sure of.

She suspected that an accident could have been the activity of evil spirits which had been summoned for such a task. In Liam's head his wife had put an evil spell on him and June deduced that it was possible. Pity welled up in her heart for him, because he appeared to be so fearful of his wife's powers.

They sat quietly for a few minutes. His loyal devotee wanted to comfort him, but was not sure what to say or do.

She broke the silence, suddenly, by uttering quietly,

'Liam, what do you think of Jesus Christ?'

Not sure why such a question had popped into her mind, she determined to hold him at ransom and get an answer from him. The curious girl suspected that such a question was relevant to her as, the night before she had listened to her mother's pensive ramblings about the person of Jesus. Mother believed that Jesus was God come in the flesh and that there was only one God who revealed Himself through the Father, Son and Holy Spirit. That alone was difficult to understand, she had to admit.

Liam winced at the name.

'Do you think He's God's Son?' she asked, soldiering on with her inquiry.

She genuinely wanted to know what he thought, seeing that he *was her* spiritual guide.

He seemed quite shaken by the direct question, especially since he had worked so hard to indoctrinate the compliant little soul, into total rejection of Judeo-Christian beliefs.

Sitting up straight momentarily, he suddenly looked taller, and he resolved to choose his words carefully, being slightly concerned that he could be losing the loyalty of his young adherent. After a long pause, he eventually answered,

'god is always evolving, and we ourselves are evolving into gods.'

'I know that' answered June, totally unaware of the displeasure he was feeling.

'*But* do you think Jesus is the God that created us, I mean?'

Again, there was a poignant moment of silence as Liam chose his words carefully. In a calculating way he answered.

'There are many gods and many roads that lead to [xxxv]Nirvana....well, I better be off.'

He scrambled to his feet, grasping for his crutches. Visibly shaken, he did not wait for June to escort him to the door and he made a quick exit. June was perplexed at his sudden departure. What had she done wrong and would she see him again?

Strangely enough, she did not see him again. In his flurry to get away, he did not even give June instructions on what to do with the many books which he had lent her.

It seemed that Liam and his wife completely disappeared off the face of the earth, although the rumour was, that they had gone to Australia. There were still so many questions that she wanted to ask him. How could he have just left her in the lurch like that? She came to the conclusion that her inquiring mind had led her down a road that Liam was not willing to go. It seemed repulsive to him to even think that there could be one God who desired to have a personal relationship with His creation by entering the arena of the world and becoming a human being Himself. That seemed too simple.

On the other hand Eastern mysticism was so complicated, the more complicated the more true it must be, she deduced in her more confused moments. She admitted that there was a desperate need within her to have a guide who would help her to wade through the mysteries of it all.

Grant it, [xxxvi]Lob sang Rampa's writings were about the easiest of the readings, but after that it seemed that the literature became a hazy mass of riddles.

It felt like she had been caught in a spider's web, except that the web had no centre and she was getting dizzy going round and round trying to find it.

Perhaps the receiving of the [xxxvii]*Third Eye* which Lobsang Rampa spoke about would illuminate her soul, she mused, or maybe there was another way to grasp the third eye concept, through the 6th sense possibly? That was part of the occultist camp she realized..... Yes...it would be the simpler way to go. Her mind was suddenly, taking her down avenues that spoke of desperation. She pondered on her train of thought which had brought her to such a conclusion and made her way to the book shelf. Reaching out for a formidable work on the practices of the Occult, she made a new resolution. It was to read the book from cover to cover and explore seriously the realm of the occult....After all, Liam did stress that all roads led to spiritual enlightenment and to be frank it seemed that Liam's wife had got the knack of it.

*** *

On the other hand life at college wasn't going too well. June was finding less and less time to do her school work thanks to her commitment to finding Jimmy and her pursuits and exploits in spiritual enlightenment. The only subject that she enjoyed was Art and she had a certain flare for it. But Maths well, that was another story. She blamed the tutor for her lack of interest and understanding.

'He talks to himself as he scribbles endless equations on the blackboard and gets irritated when someone asks a question. At that point, the poor, lost soul of a student gets scolded for not keeping up.' whined June to her friend Rachel.

Rachel was aware that the 'poor, lost soul' June alluded to was more often than not, June herself. Being the diplomatic young lady that she was, Rachel would make all the right noises but it was obvious to her, that her friend had lost her way in class.

After her ordeal with Shane, Rachel had prepared a mandate for herself and it was, to one day, take over her father's lucrative business. Woe to anyone who tried to distract her from her objective! So, if necessary she would have to leave her long time friend behind. It was not her fault that her mate was an under achiever and it was imperative to move on without June, if needs be.

***

When it came to literature though... Mr. Scott seemed to be digging a political grave for himself. Where it was all going to end no one was sure. The intrigue was escalating within the classroom environment as Mr. Scott's point of view progressively intensified.

Eventually it climaxed one day in a march down the main street with his students wielding gay right and anti apartheid placards. Besides his stand against apartheid, the issue of gay rights was one of his pet ideologies and it was his answer to the over population in the world.

His pathetic little class looked quite a spectacle, as they wandered aimlessly down the street in same sex pairs. Although the students were slightly puzzled about where the connection was made between gay rights and his passion for anti apartheid ideas, they didn't question it, as their escape from the classroom was a treat that deserved participation in any demonstration.

Unfortunately Mr. Scott's aim in getting his student's interested in their same sex partners backfired, when it came to June, because it was during the demonstraton that June met Nick, a Jewish boy, who made her laugh out loud all the time.

CHAPTER 23

"Purple haze all in my eyes
don't know if it's day or night
you've got me blowin', blowin' my mind
is it tomorrow or just the end of time"
Jimi Hendrix

This colliding of the kindred spirits, led to a happy consolidation of friendship, which evolved into a romance, followed by the inevitable meeting of the family on both sides.

So, when June was introduced to Nick's doting mother she was slightly puzzled at the delight the woman expressed, concerning her son's choice of romantic pursuit and in a flurry of hospitality, June found herself the centre of attention within the family.

In her moments of resolution, June had promised herself that she would not hang around with anyone who went to college with her. Even Rachel, who was officially her best friend, fell into this category. But lately, to escape her present group of friends, she had become a bit more lenient, concerning this situation and dared to break the current rule by swallowing her pride and reviewing her former resolution.

Nick was not very religious, when it came to Judaism, but like the majority of his kin he had a great sense of humour and was making it his ambition to follow a career in stand up comedy. His avid fan club consisted of one young girl who was content to spend her time laughing at his jokes.

It was like a breath of fresh air, hanging out with Nick. No longer was anxiety and worry an issue to her. She did not have to anticipate her evenings ending in a paranoid obsession, that the police were after her and her friends. Nor did she have to participate in the culture of suspicion involving police informants among their group and she enjoyed an interval from the prospects of her friends doing something weird and stupid while tripping out on LSD.

It seemed that Nick had no vices.... well, none that were too serious she thought and they spent many a night reading Shakespeare together. At times like these, the passionate youth would collapse in the middle of some highly emotional paragraph and June would find herself peering down at him from her bed as he lay dramatically on the floor in a heap at the end of a turbulent scene.

***

Just as Nick and June were getting to know each other and the relationship had progressed to the place where Nick was looking for a whole new set of jokes to keep the amused girl content, Jimmy appeared, unexpectedly at the door.

He looked down at her and smiled his crooked smile, revealing the enchanting dimple on the right side of his cheek. His brown eyes twinkled with confidence and he was quite sure that his smitten consort would allow him entrance back into her life.

She opened the door wide for him. His crew cut and pallid countenance spoke volumes to her. He had either been in hospital or prison. It was not necessary to ask him, as she was aware that he was reluctant when it came to answering questions. Anyway, she was sure that in due time he would give her a glimpse into the window of his soul. There was no hurry....her idol had returned...nothing else really mattered.

The relationship soon thickened into a cauldron of apprehension for her mother. And Jimmy's frequent visits fuelled the fires of anxiety and concern on the part of her parents.

'Mum, I'm going with Jimmy to his parent's house today, so don't be worried if we're a bit late home.'

Declared the excited teenager, as she flung the front door opened and rushed out, doing her best to avoid any eye contact with her mother. She could not help herself, absence had only made her heart grow fonder and here he was in the flesh waiting for her downstairs. A little flustered at her own behaviour, June forced all thoughts of her mother out of her mind. There was an adventure waiting for her and her rascally escort and she was happy at last.

***

Jimmy's parents lived in an idyllic, country environment, which was a stark contrast to the inner city dwelling which June resided in.

Close to their home was a stream which ran through the nearby forest and the enjoyable afternoon was spent wading in the water and collecting pure clay, which was perfect for pottery making.

The lazy day passed pleasantly, and June relished every moment of it. There was no signs of Jimmy lighting up a joint of marijuana. Talk of getting high was not mentioned by him and June pensively wondered whether his mysterious absence had somehow liberated and empowered him to kick the habit. She scolded herself for even thinking such a reckless and amazing thought . To imagine that he had actually turned over a new leaf, was more than she could fathom.

Her thoughts continued to unravel and she asked herself the inevitable question, 'why am I head over heels in love with this young man? Is it just his good looks?' The inquiry led her to the issue of her weaknesses. One of them being that she 'was a sucker for a pretty face', as the saying goes. It definitely wasn't his stimulating conversation, she mused conclusively.

She felt a tinge of annoyance at the compliance that manifested in her. Why she was as submissive to him, as the clay that they had just collected from the river bed, was beyond her understanding. There was also a niggling feeling in the pit of her stomach that she had lost control and was under some sort of spell. The gates of her soul had obviously been wrenched opened by the lad... but could she lay the blame completely on him?.... had she not participated willingly in the process and with very little struggle? The question was .... How would she ever retrieve her soul?.

By his confident gait and as she straddled a little behind him, he communicated through his body language his awareness of the power that he usurped over her. He was altogether beguiling to her, even though he had lost more weight off his already, slim body. As her mother would have described him, if she had been fond of him, he was a *satin bag of bones* and what beautiful bones they were.

***

Jimmy's mother had prepared a meal and the evening started on a good footing within a context of harmonious fellowship.   Then something went seriously wrong somewhere along the way.

An atmosphere of tension proceeded to evolve just under the surface of the polite conversation which was taking place around the table.   Even the preplexed guest, felt like a volcano was just about to erupt and it dawned upon the young lady at the table, that her darling villain had brought her to that place with ulterior motives.   She was, without doubt, his peace token to his parents.   It was obvious that this was his first time home since his being away and to cushion the onslaught of anger, June had been summoned.

'You know Bill the mechanic?' began Jimmy's dad, between mouthfuls of food. Jimmy did not look up, but responded with a grunt, recognizing that the conversation could escalate out of control.

'Well, he's looking for help in his garage, and he's willing to give you a chance to work with him.' His Dad looked intently at his son, hoping to get his attention. But Jimmy did not return the eye contact.

'Son, if you want to stay out of trouble...... you need to work' continued the older man who was containing himself as amicably as possible.

There was little response from his wayward son, who continued to thrust food into his mouth, and then out of the blue, asked

'Hey ma, what's for desert?'

He looked up suddenly from his dinner and grinned a rascally smile at his mother. Awkwardly she pushed the chair back and disappeared into the kitchen.

'Did you hear what I said to you?' Mr. Jackson asked slowly, with controlled restraint.

At last Jimmy responded.

'Ah dad, lets not talk about this now, we have a guest.'

'Well, when will we talk about it, tell me that, when?...listen here, now is your opportunity to own your own car, instead of going out and stealing one!.' His dad was not going to let the subject lay dormant any longer. Now was as good a time as any.

'Ah no, not now!' came the exasperated reply.

Mr. Jackson opened his mouth to say something else but was cut short by Mrs. Jackson who hollowed from the kitchen.

'Yes Dad leave it for now...you know the medium told us that Jimmy was going to steal a car and end up in prison...so just let it be.'

'What are you talking about' exclaimed Mr. Jackson.

'Don't you remember the séance that Jimmy was present at...you remember.... his fourteenth birthday. Well, Serita saw it all in a vision, even to the colour of the car. We should have known that this was coming..... its fate...is it not?'

Jimmy's Dad shook his head in exasperation. He had suddenly lost his appetite his knife and fork clattered onto the plate and he sat stiffly in his chair.

'Those séances, were terrible things, we should never have started attending the spiritualist church. But never mind that, Jim, you have to think of your future!'

He said pounding the table with his fist.

'Ah Dad, stop nagging,' came the retort, as Jimmy sprung from his seat and escaped into the kitchen.

'Come back here young man!' The older man demanded.

June could hear Jimmy in the kitchen, tormenting his mother. He was saying something about 'Acid'.... aaaaaaccccccccid nya ha ha...aaaaccccccid nya ha ha.

'Whats he saying' asked his Dad, who was puzzled, and out of his depth with his son's behaviour.

'Get out of the kitchen..right now...' cried his mother. Flustered and bewildered she began to push him out of the kitchen.

He returned to the lounge and repeated what he was saying in the kitchen.

'Acccccid, Accccid   Ha ha ha....Accccid'   his ramblings grew louder and evolved into incoherent hissing that was strangely eerie.

Just as the tension was at its height his parents solved the problem by simply ignoring him. The following solution was to send him and his poor companion on their way as soon as possible.

It did not take the opinion of an expert to observe, that there was a history behind the present dynamics in the family's behaviour. In the past, such conversations must have had disastrous results. June recoiled as she imagined what the outcomes of past conflicts must've looked like.

Failing to confront the issue successfully, Mr Jackson decided that the next best thing was to take the path of least resistance and dispose quickly of his tormentors. Without hesitation he grabbed the keys off the mantle piece and whisked the wayward young couple to wherever destination they felt disposed to go.

It did not take long for the flustered parent to release his prodigal son and the girl out onto the street. June looked back to wave goodbye, but Jimmy's dad had already pulled off and was driving away. She felt dazed at what had happened and looked up at her boyfriend for reassurance that everything was alright. It was as if he didn't care at all about anything. There was no sign of remorse or regret at what had just transpired. The beautiful side to evil was manifesting before her very eyes.

***

As the days went by June noticed that Jimmy did not know how to express himself at all on any level. It was as if he had got lost down some dark corridor and couldn't be found or reached. At times, June was tempted to call down the deep recesses of his mind and spirit and command the real Jimmy to present himself, because the person that was resident within him, she was certain, was not him. She imagined him as a little boy. How sweet he must've been. She had been given a glimpse into what had transpired between his childhood and his early youth. Had something dark and sinister taken over this lad during those séances? She wondered. She could only speculate.

Then one night, his restlessness was too much for June, and she felt the need to do something outlandish to get his attention, even if it was negative attention, she didn't care anymore. The moment arose, when he started expressing his dislike for her taste in music, by throwing one LP after another across the room as if they were frizbees.

She squatted at the top of the bed and watched him patiently. He lay across her feet and pursued his activity with no concern. Suddenly, he paused in his distasteful occupation and pulled J*esus Christ Super Star* out of the pile. She was suddenly curious at what was running through his mind. He scowled glumly at the unfamiliar record cover, trying to retrieve any connection with it and seizing the opportunity, at that moment, June bent over him and whispered in his pixie like ear.

'Jimmy what do you think of Jesus Christ?'

To her surprise, he immediately dropped the record on the floor. It made a clattering noise as it fell out of the cover. Without looking at her, he slid off the bed and began to wriggle his way out of the room on his

150

belly, as if he was in a war zone, under heavy fire. The wriggling along the floor progressed to a leopard crawl and at last he got to his feet, grabbed his things and ran out the of the apartment.

June got off the bed and stood aghast at the bedroom door. She could not make head or tail of what had just happened.

'Why was it that she kept doing that?' was her first thought.

She had succeeded once more, in chasing the love of her life out of her home and possibly she would not see him again. He had escaped and knowing Jimmy, that would be the end of him for a very long time. Her eyes filled with tears and she wondered if she should go after him, but he would be well down the road by the time she pulled herself together.

The distressed girl gathered up her thoughts and sat at the dining room table, thankful that her parents had been out, but now, wished that they would come home. She felt frightened. Jimmy had reminded her of a snake. The way he slithered along the floor... had that really happened? Was it physically possible to move in that manner? Perhaps she had imagined it all. Oh how she wished it had been a figment of her imagination.

Suddenly the door opened and in walked her parents. Their light chatter about the evening dissolved the feeling of darkness that had settled over her. She had never been so happy to see them. It was evident to her mother that something had occurred while they had been out. The tense look in her daughter's face, was enough to let her know that it was best not to ask after the whereabouts of Jimmy. She knew instinctively that he would not be around again for a very long time.

CHAPTER 24

'I feel the ice in my head
Running its hands through my bed.'
Deep purple 1968

It was in Nick's arms that June eventually found comfort. The relationship was resumed where it left off and no questions were asked.

June should have felt secure with Nick, after all he prided himself in being a good Jewish boy and his mother thought the world of him.

Seeing each other at college everyday strengthened their relationship and they prided themselves in being a cut above most of the youth in the community. Or rather, they had more money than the regular 'Joe blog' in the street. It puzzled June to think that her parents were paying so much money for her to get educated when in reality she was spending an awful lot of time in the corridors cuddling her boyfriend and taking long smoke breaks out in the street. Her feeling of security soon vanished, when, after being introduced to Nick's mates it became a weekend routine to attend private viewings of X rated movies.

'Where are you taking me tonight?' asked June hesitantly, ruminating whether she should mount his bike and venture out with him. In her frustration, she had let him know on more than one occasion that sleazy films were not enjoyable to her, even though his argument was that he was educating her in all things sexual.

'No, tonight is different.' He replied, 'we're going to a party.' That sounded a bit better than the outings that he had arranged for the past few weekends.

'It better be a good one' she said under her breath, as she put on her helmet and jumped on the back of the bike.

'Oh yes, it will be' came the answer as he pulled off at full speed, keen to get to his destination.

When they arrived at the party, June wondered why there were no girls present. There were only boys sitting around the lounge. What was the attraction? They all seemed so animated and alive? She felt an uneasiness inside her as she made her way to a corner of the room and snuggled into a bean bag, while her sociable boyfriend mingled with his mates, and chortled noisily at unheard comments that the surly boys were making.

Where were the snacks, the drinks, the music? She wondered. Suspiciously, she surveyed the scene and soon supposed a pattern of movement in operation.... a boy looking very pleased with himself would appear from the back room and another one would take his place and disappear into the same back room. What was in the backroom? This was all new to June.

Finally, after a gruelling evening of watching all the boys coming and going from what June assumed, was the bedroom, a very young, dishevelled girl with flaming red hair stepped out of the darkened room. She hesitated at the doorway and glanced at June sitting in the corner. Their eyes met for a moment. A hint of shame was in the red head's glance, and as if embarrassed, she dropped her eyes to the floor and disappeared into the bathroom.

June felt suddenly sick.

'That's it, its over between us! You can't even take me to a normal party!' ......What point are you trying to make!' she hollered as she leapt off the bike and removed her helmet. Her hair tumbled, precariously down her back and over her shoulders. Unpertubed by the outburst, Nick launched into his rehearsed argument.

'The point is that you need educating, you can't stay a virgin all your life you know!....don't you want to be different, *all* the girls are virgins ...why don't *you* be different!' June looked at him curiously, thinking how totally absurd his argument was and began to giggle. Teetering on the brink of hysteria, she answered sarcastically,

'Yeh, like the fifteen year old red head. Oh yes I'm sure she's a virgin.....One thing I am sure of ... she's a Gentile like me! You wouldn't treat one of your Jewish girlfriends like that now would you?'

She turned away from him with an air of finality and strided through the foyer of the building, swinging the helmet carelessly at her side.

As the lift door closed behind her, she felt a tinge of regret, that she had hurled an argument at him that had a discriminatory element to it, but besides that, she felt fully within her rights to express her feelings, and she was glad that she did so. She had to give him his due, he had gone to great lengths to seduce her, but all his tactics, had back fired completely. She thought back to their relationship together and remembered him whispering in her ear something like,

'A woman is like a beautiful fruit ...you peal away the skin until you get to the juicy flesh within'. Was his favourite line.

In those intimate moments the desperate youth, would attempt to charm her with such poetic reflections, ever conscious of his simmering frustration. Her silly naivity, which was ever present, would cause her to gaze into his eyes as they reclined together on the bed....but that was all....it only became a revelation to her at that moment of reflection, that she had played a major part in making him the wretch that he had presently become. Not willing to admit her part in creating a monster, she continued to stir up the feeling of resentment that she had first felt.

'How could he have used such tasteless tactics to try and seduce me?' she mused defensively.

'He should have stuck to poetry and humour...it would have had a much better effect at the "pealing away" process...eventually', she concluded, as she poured herself a very bubbly bath, with the intent of spending a lot of time soaking, until she felt squeaky clean.

'I guess I do send out conflicting signals.' She admitted to herself as she slid into the warm bubbles.

***

The outcome of all this was that June decided that actually, she felt more at home and had more fun with her original group of friends. They were poor and unfortunate, yet in an odd sort of way, they were genuine. Grant it they had a drug problem, but June felt that there was a certain philosophy and depth to their drug consumption which deserved some recognition. She reckoned that she would rather be with her *druggy* friends, than with the privileged dudes who had enough money to adopt more sophisticated vices, that were, frankly, in June's eyes, more evil.

So consequently, evenings were from then on, spent lying around the stereo set. It was Bugsy's job to move the music on by jolting the record player with his foot. In their doped up state, at times no one would notice that the record had been stuck in a groove for half an hour until Bugsy resumed his former duty.

156

'Rather the devil you know than the devil you don't' she decided.

The problem was that nothing stays the same, and that meant that June's long time friends had also changed, some were descending deeper into the drug culture and had discovered heroine. Grant it they were presently taking it orally and smoking it, but in June's mind and from her limited experience of observation, it would not be long before they were *mainlining* and she could not bear to see her friends do that. She had to admit, also, that there was an ever present fear within her that she would be convinced to follow her friends into such a terrible habit if she did not save herself somehow.

It was all too much to cope with.

Rumours had emerged from friends in Johannesburg, about their peers, whose veins had collapsed from injecting too often, and in desperation, did things like bathe in painfully hot baths to try and swell the veins, or *spike* into their groins or feet as a last resort.

This information, had left June floundering in alarm and fright.

***

Fortunately, it was around this time that her mother sensed that her sullen daughter needed some sort of an incentive to get her concentrating on her studies. Time was short and her matric exams were only a few months away.

'After you've done your matric, your dad and I have decided to take you back to England for a holiday, so it's important that you pass your exams, so that you can enjoy the trip.' She announced.

Her mother's well planned speech resulted in June putting her mystical books aside and listlessly getting down to her school work.

As time went by, she justified the fact that comparing sacred religious writings had something to do with English literature, and so, many evenings of study were spent, doing just that..... comparing religions. It was fascinating, to ponder on the Hindu scriptures from the Bhagavagita and then compare them with the Koran, but what she found more interesting than all of that, was the power that one little Bible verse had over all the other sacred writings. One or two lines from the Bible, profoundly affected her.

It was during one of these times that she stumbled upon a saying of Jesus...He said [xxxviii]'*If you seek you will find*'.. It occurred to her, at that point that... yes, she was 'seeking', what it was, in reality that was being sought for, was still a mystery to her, but the heartening words of the Guru Jesus gave her hope that she would find what she was looking for.

Curiously she was also fascinated by the way that Jesus said that [xxxix]He was the truth. If that was so, then there was only one absolute truth and it was all wrapped up in Him. How simple was that! No more wading around in copious amounts of philosophical ideas, like a blind man trying to feel his way around a very large maze.

Although she was working through all these issues, she felt better about her school work, when she saw an occasional poetry or maths book jutting out from the pile of otherwise irrelevant books, strewn across her bed.

At this present time, she seldom left the house and had given her mother a list of people that she didn't want to see. It was her mother's task to make excuses on June's behalf and she relished the idea that the studious youth was alone and safe in her room, studying...so she thought.

The only people that got over the threshold to see June was Nick and his new boyfriend. This distracted June long enough to try and fathom how the signs had been missed, that Nick was actually bisexual . Her assumption was that Mr. Scott's ideas had gained a willing follower after all, how many more had he influenced? June didn't have the time at that point, to reflect.

It was only after the exams that this question was answered. Her perturbed parents had discovered that she had failed her exams miserably. They had hunted in the daily paper, and could not find her name among those who had successfully graduated. So they waited for the report to come and quietly gave her the letter to open. The news was conveyed to her that way.

Mr Scott's influence suddenly pushed its way to the foreground of June's muddled mind as she leant precariously over the edge of the wall, looking down at the eleven floors below her, where she remembered seeing the lifeless body of the little girl, who had plummeted from the floors above her. The gloomy memories invoked a feeling that she should end it all by jumping. After all Mr. Scott had pummelled into his students heads, the idea that it was not worth living if they didn't get their matric.

'You might as well commit suicide' he had asserted recklessly, on more than one occasion.

What did her future hold? Without a Matric certificate, there was not much she could do with her life. What was life all about anyway? Weariness welled up within her and she felt years older than her seventeen, tender years. A sudden swathe of self hatred enveloped her, and although the feeling was overwhelming, she could not let herself go in that way. Anyhow, heights were an issue to her.

'Not today.' She decided, perhaps another time and in another way that wouldn't be so messy she resolved. She humoured herself by laying hold of the thought that perhaps her dad would like to throw her over the balcony instead. 'After all she had squandered his money on her futile studies.'

The element of humour helped her to shrug off her darkening frame of mind. She lifted her heavy eyes to the horizon and looked into the distance at the massive cruisers and cargo ships, docked in the harbour.

Crains jutted out along the skyline, loading and unloading cargo, twenty four hours a day. The never ending bustle of business, the creaking of rusty metal. The loud bellow from ship funnels, as they left the harbour for a far away coastline, comforted June and with new eyes she feasted on the scene that was just beyond her doorway. She took a deep breath and crept back inside. With tear stained eyes, she faced her parents but no one said anything, and life went on as usual.

***

'So what does FF stand for?' wondered June, when she finally plucked up enough courage to look more closely at her marks. The document was displayed the F, E, E, and D symbols in that order but one of the symbols was 'FF'? She took a long drag of her cigarette, which stung her lips. Forming smoke rings in the humid air, she answered her own question by saying, 'I guess it stands for *fucking* failure!'. The piece of paper was promptly screwed up and briskly thrown into the dustbin. It bounced off the edge of the bin and landed on the floor. With a sigh, she lay back down on Andy's hairy chest.

Andy had mellowed over the years, and had long ago, traded his little beetle in for a more substantial vehicle. He had become a diplomatic fellow, who thought it wise only to chuckle at the comment.

He had always been there for her in the background and usually turned up between chapters in her life, lingering more often as of late. Their relationship was purely plutonic and it was comfortable being around him because she didn't have to put on any aires or graces. He was part of the depleting circle of friends that she still had, those who accepted her for who she was. Though prone to a hardened heart, due to what life was churning up, she was learning to cherish the few friends that she had left and was grateful for her secure home life. These two factors in her life helped to refine her outlook on life ....slightly.

CHAPTER 25

Break another little piece
Of my heart, now darling!
Janis Joplin 1963

The black and red funnel of the Union castle liner
bellowed loudly over the harbour, as the big ship
slowly left the dock. June stood on deck and waved
goodbye to her friend Andy. She was excited to be
leaving Durban and all its problems.

In the distance she could see the block of flats
where she lived. How many hours had been spent
looking out at the harbour, could not be counted, but
now the scenery had been reversed.

Her thoughts lingered on the last, significant
images that reminded her of Durban. Little Ken's
vacant expression after an acid trip, (although he wasn't
so little anymore, as, at last, he had grown into a
handsome youth) but, in June's mind, he personified
the drug culture.

Then there was the newspaper article about Mr.
Scott, who had managed to whip up the fury of the
local Nationalist Party to the point where they
succeeded in blowing up his car. Whether it was an
attempted murder no-one knew, but the message was
loud and clear and Mr. Scott left the country soon after
the incident.

Drugs and politics was what she wanted to escape
from. England was her means of escape. In
anticipation she had packed her portfolio of paintings
with the hope of being accepted into an art college.

She guessed that she was being a bit naive, but there was still a flicker of hope and she could only try and be optimistic. Her plan was to spend lots of time on deck, looking out to sea and plotting her future. What an idyllic pastime! She thought, as her thoughts brightened slightly.

Life on board was not something new to June. It was her mother's favourite form of transporting them from country to country in search of a land to settle. On the other hand, her dad preferred flying and would go ahead of them, by air, to prepare a home, so that by the time the family reached their destination, they could settle into their new surroundings immediately. Consequently, they had evolved into seasoned travellers and at those specific times, the family were prompted to remember the patriarch's favourite quotes,

'The only luggage you need when travelling is a tooth brush in your back pocket' followed by,

'With possessions you will be possessed.' Hence the presence of very few belongings.

But there was another reason, why he liked to fly, rather than travel by ship. It was when June was very little, when travelling by sea from Kenya to England, her dad had got into a scuffle with a young deck hand who had expressed his interests in the young, attractive Mandy. This had resulted in her Dad swearing at him in a strange language, to be more precise.... Swahili. This odd behaviour had become a traditional, family joke.

'If you're going to swear, Roy, swear in Swahili, so that no one can understand you.' Mother would say, whenever he was frustrated with something.

Unfortunately, it looked like history was going to repeat itself, as it did not take long for June to meet a member of the crew. Their casual daily greeting developed into a friendship and escalated from there into a holiday romance. In the back of her mind she had resolved to follow in her big sister's footsteps.

Rab was a Glaswegian. He had beautiful black curls that decked his well formed shoulders. His glorious eyes, reflected the blueness of the sea and his accent was mysterious and romantic. The only problem was that June could understand very little of what he was saying.

It all culminated one night in total confusion, when a mishap of communication, saw June go ashore, in the Canaries, with her new found friends. She didn't realize that she was supposed to be meeting Rab at that specific hour.

So, when she returned, the whole ship was talking about the young 'deckie' who had tried to commit suicide. It was Rab. He was taken ashore by the ambulance and June was afraid that she would never see him again. Torrents of tears followed and every effort was made to try and locate him, but to no avail. All she could do was leave a forwarding address and hope that he would somehow get hold of her.

'Oh how exciting!' exclaimed June's grandmother, when they eventually reached Southampton.

'Did you fall into his arms and give him the kiss of life?' she inquired with a humorous sparkle in her eye.

'No, this isn't the story of sleeping beauty in reverse' answered June bluntly, aware that her granny wasn't seeing the scenario in a serious enough light for her liking, but how could she expect anything else from *this* nanny, seeing that all social problems were summed in her favourite quotation,

'The best way to get friends is to put a bottle of brandy on the coffee table.' And at that present moment June had no sense of humour .

It was when they reached the Isle of Sheppey and visited the other grandparents that emotions ran high.

A letter arrived and with great trepidation June opened it, hoping it was from Rab, but it was not to be, as Andy's spider like writing looked forlornly back at June from the page. Through the tears she reluctantly read what he had to say and could not contain her pain at the unfolding information it contained. Kenny had decided to stay in Durban and not return to Cape Town where he had been living in a commune with a group of hippies. That meant that if she returned to Durban she would have to stumble across his handsome but distressing person and all that he represented....she could not go back there. The letter suddenly turned into a handkerchief and she blew her nose on it. It distressed her that she felt such strongly negative emotions for the boy that she had grown up with, who was now a man with gentle green eyes.

Eventually, a letter from Rab did arrive and out dropped a photograph of him baring his bandaged wrist. He was leaning against a tree with an ominous looking hospital in the background.

The great day arrived when they met each other, once again. Dramatically they ran into each other's arms and promised never ending love to one another.

The euphoria soon faded though, when June realized that Rab passionately, hated the English. She was familiar with the conflict that often raged between the Afrikaner and the English in the South African context but was out of her depth when it came to the strong feelings between the Scottish and the English. She felt it wise to try and ditch the agitator, being the new comer that she was. But that would be easier said than done, since she felt obligated to devote herself to the disturbed young man. So there were moments during the day where she pretended that she didn't know the very vocal man who was at sporadic moments, verbally abusing, some unfortunate English passerby in the

165

street. It was a relief to eventually detach herself from his very intense presence, by bidding him farewell from the platform, as his train left the station from London, back to Scotland.

***

On a cold blustering March afternoon, she sat with her mother on a damp bench overlooking the grey, mist ridden sea.

'I think I'm going to commit suicide.' June declared sadly. There was silence.

Mother cleared her throat and answered as wisely as she could, by making light of the comment.

'Well, you will have to wait until you're eighteen, to do that, because you are still under age.'

June was speechless, and pondered on what she had just said to her mother.

What did being eighteen have to do with committing suicide?.... perhaps her mother had not heard her correctly, and thought she had said, ' I want to apply for my driver's license.' She felt like repeating herself but the moment had passed. She slouched down into her scarf and coat and pouted sulkily. Life was churning up some ludicrous rubbish, she thought glumly.

***

June could only imagine the conversation that went on between her parents that night, because the next day the decision was made that she was going with her father to Canada to see her uncle and cousins and her mother was escaping to Ireland for a well earned rest from her difficult teenager.

One of her three Canadian cousins was the same age as her. She remembered him as a chubby kid, who tormented her incessantly with general knowledge questions. This did not help her, as a little girl, whose feelings of insecurity were running high. Canada had been a very different place to what she was used to in East Africa and only two years into settling there, her father decided that the cold weather was not for him and it was decided that South Africa was going to be their next and final destination.

But now, six years later, against the backdrop of an old established school, Rodney her cousin, a lean young man sauntered up to her. The transformation had been complete. Clad in a Scottish Kilt, June had to admit that he was aesthetically pleasing to the eye and it was evident that he felt the same way about her.

He also turned out to be the school's dealer in all things drug orientated. This meant that much time was spent searching for his illusive keys that always disappeared deep, inside his heavy overcoat, jacket or jeans and so in a spaced out frame of mind, it became a novel experience trying to retrieve them.

Being high on hash also meant that visiting Toronto to look up her old friend who turned out to be an ageing border collie, named Stormy, who, June insisted still remembered her as that little girl who used to take him for his daily runs in the park, became top of the list of things to do while in Canada. She had also bought a pack of Tarot cards and Rodney was her first customer to hear what the future held for him.

It did not take her long to fall out of favour with all things Canadian, when, one day she was invited out by a young man who was a friend of the family. His intention was to show her the beautiful countryside. So, as they cruised through the forests in his big Rover, with [xl]*Dead skunk in the middle of the road* playing in

167

the background, she flicked her lit cigarette butt nonchalantly out of the window, as one does in Africa.... bush fires not being as big a deal as it is in the forests of Canada. Suddenly, the driver slammed the brakes on, sprang from the car and pounced upon the embers of the cigarette. With passion, he killed it a hundred times over. At once, the tour ended and she was immediately taken home like a naughty child and was dispensed with to a responsible adult.

The disfavour deepened when she found herself exposed to the Canadian education system. She was invited as a guest speaker to be interrogated by a large assembly of 6th formers. Notorious South Africa was the topic.

All eyes were on her, as questions were fired one after another. Her answers were all the same.

'We don't want the Communists in the country.' She felt it safe just to echo her dad's words and elaborated by adding, [xli]'We have the Cubans on the borders and our borders need to be protected.'

At the point when she thought she was doing quite well, a bright young man with thick glasses drawled.

'What are your personal views on *segregation?*'

The term was unfamiliar to June and she was admittedly stumped by what she sensed was a 'get to the heart of the matter' question. She twiddled a lock of hair between her fingers, nervously and for a moment hesitated, shrugged her shoulders and answered wretchedly, 'If it keeps communism at bay.... then cool.'

Very definitely, that was the wrong answer, as a gasp rose from the assembly. Her ears began to redden and her freckles darkened against the spot lights.

'Do you have those who inform on the situation?' Came the next question.

By this time June was totally disorientated.

Recognizing the word *inform she* answered in a panic, 'Oh yes we have many informers' and as was a spur of the moment reaction, she giggled nervously, as her thoughts darted from the political situation to the drug culture. She hoped and prayed that a student or two, would catch onto her line of thought and steer the majority of interrogators away from the subject of politics. But to no avail. A sea of stony, expressionless faces stared up at her. The silence at that moment could have been broken by a pin dropping on the floor.

Awkwardly clearing his throat, the teacher terminated the session, by launching into a summary of *his* interpretation of the situation.

'As we can gather from what this young lady is saying,' it seems that '*a one man one vote*' situation is not possible while the right winged government is in control and revolution might be inevitable if there is not an abolition of the law of *segregation*, more commonly known as the *apartheid*.'

His sweeping statement was accentuated by a whisk of his hand as he dismissed the classes. The kids scrambled for the exit and disappeared at the sound of the siren, leaving June perched on her stool, looking silly.

June realized at that point what the spectacled boy was getting at. But it was too late the moment had passed. She could have shared Mr. Scott's experience, the attempt on his life by bombing his car and many other things that the current government got up to, if only she had grasped the meaning of a simple word *se...gre..gation*.

Meanwhile, lines were already being drawn in the political arena between the lefts and the rights and it was all dramatically unfolding down the school corridors as June glided past a group of long haired kids with ominous scowls on their faces. She

169

wondered, naively why the dark looks were aimed at her and was blissfully unaware that the youth who were escorting her safely off the premises were right wing capitalists, with fascist leanings.

A whirlwind of political debate had been ignited all around her and she didn't know how to diffuse it, as it raged amongst her peers. The majority of them saw her as an object of contempt. Being South African was not fun. She felt like a flimsy raft tossed about in a sea of controversy with no anchor, equipped with meagre knowledge of the subject. For, just managing her own life was a major task without taking on the political intrigue of South Africa as well, but oh, how she hated herself for it. She hated her passport for bearing the South African stamp in it. That alone excluded her from even stepping over the white line on the bridge between Canada and America, to get a snap of her on American soil. Why did she have to reside in a country that triggered worldwide revulsion? She could not call such a place, her home. Would she ever find her real home?

'It just goes to show how we can get our communication lines crossed' she related to Rodney as they made their way to a night club in Toronto. Rodney was not too interested in the situation in Africa and was at that moment rummaging furiously through his many pockets for a cigarette. They stood at the traffic lights while he performed the major task at hand, when a hippie sauntered up to them.

His face lighted up as he offered June a tract and muttered 'Jesus loves you'. There was a glint in his eye that spoke of sobre passion, like he really meant it and at that brief moment in time... she believed him.

CHAPTER 26

*'One thing you can't hide,
Is when you're crippled inside.'*
John Lennon *(Imagine) 1971*

The sea was choppy as the ship embarked on the long journey back to South Africa. Gazing out at the disappearing, white cliffs of the English coast, June's heart felt heavy. She had done everything in her power to remain in England. The glimmer of hope was short lived when her application into art school had been rejected. Nevertheless, her determination had led her down another path, that of attempting to change her age on her passport, making her legally old enough to get a job as a stewardess on one of the liners. Forgery was the last resort and even her mother had become a partner in the crime, but the technique was beyond them, and they soon gave up the shady project

As well as this, Rab had vowed never ending love to June, who had reciprocated reluctantly. Her positive response though, prompted him to assure her that he would be returning to the coasts of Africa as soon as he got his old job back on board. She felt uncomfortable about her commitment to him and secretly hoped that he wouldn't get his job back.

Armed with her Tarot cards, which were banned in South Africa, but were easy to smuggle into the country, she fancied herself as a fortune teller and planned to chisel out a career in the art once she returned to Durban. Her image would have to change of course. So, she proceeded to imagine herself crowned with long black hair. This would be an easy task, once she got her hands on some hair colour. To complete the picture she envisioned herself floating around in her long black cape which she purchased from Petticoat Lane and then, of course there was the poster of Christ's face which she intended to hang on her bedroom wall. It was an eerie icon and was sure to strike fearful awe into anyone who paused to look at it, as the eyes were intense and appeared to follow the viewer around, and then at another angle the eyes would appear closed. Superstitiously, she assured herself that such an image would sanctify everything she did in her psychic activities.

***

It must have been the high stilettos and the short mini skirt that June wore to the interview that caused the prudish matron to reject her from entering the nursing profession.

After this there was a spate of other jobs. The most disastrous one being the Massage parlour. After two weeks of training to be a masseur at the hands of a middle aged man of doubtful reputation, the actual job only lasted one night but even if she hadn't been rescued by her street wise sister, who was on holiday from Rhodesia at the time, she would have got the sack soon enough for being rude to the clients who were curiously enough all men asking for sexual favours. After slamming the phone down numerous times, it suddenly dawned on June that she was working for a glorified brothel. She was relieved when Mandy, her sister stepped over the threshold into the semi lit reception room. Glancing around at the posters, she summed the scene up within a moment, and said resolutely, 'Come on we're out of here. Get your things.'

June asked no questions but picked up her bag and quit immediately.'

Then there was the job with the police. She felt like a ghost walking around the office and walked out of the job the day the political riots broke out. It was then that June found herself looking out of the window at all the desperate black people wanting their rights, as they pounded on the doors of the central police station. This was not for her. She did not want to be on the side of the oppressors, and really didn't want to die at the hands of the oppressed. If she was going to die, she wanted to orchestrate it and that was never too far from her mind, as she grew more and more disillusioned with life.

Unfortunately the struggle for independence demanded that she have a job of some sort. The bottom line was that she needed money. The Tarot reading was going well, but it was not at all lucrative. Her readings were uncannily accurate, yet she just didn't have the heart to ask for money from her clients, especially since most of them were friends of hers. Going back to school was out of the question. There was a black cloud over the college, anyway, because one of the students had actually followed through with Mr. Scott's advice and thrown herself out of the fourth floor window of the college just a few weeks after the school master was deported.

Anyway her parents couldn't bail out all that money again, and she certainly wasn't going back to public school. There seemed to be no solution to her personal plight. It seemed like she was between a rock and a hard place.

Then one evening, she stripped off all her clothes and jewellery and beheld herself in the mirror. She had spent the night in a frenzy, dancing with hundreds of other revellers, at a rock concert, yet she felt lonelier than ever. The fact that the lead singer got off the stage to dance with her, did not help her mood to recover from its decent into the abyss. Eventually, the feeling of distress and turmoil, caused her to run out of the concert in tears.

So there she stood beholding her trembling form once more. She did not care anymore that her body was not perfect or that her eyebrows, in a certain light punctuated the ginger gene that she had unfortunately inherited. All she wanted was to know herself, to be able to remove the masks. She yearned for something genuine and truthful and it seemed like some intense and invisible entity was holding her hostage and had her in a corner. Escape seemed impossible from the jealous and all pervading presence.

In desperation and for the first time, she cried out to God to help her. Life seemed so empty, what was she going to do for the rest of it. If God didn't come up with something, well, then it was not worth living anymore.

CHAPTER 27

'Smoke on the water, it seemed like we would lose the race,
Smoke on the water, fire in the sky.' Deep Purple
1972

She hesitated in her footsteps at the sight of a familiar figure coming towards her. There was no escape, he had already seen her. Acknowledging him would be the only way to make light of the, hopefully, brief encounter. Her plan was to terminate the meeting as soon as possible. For a few weeks, Ken had persisted in trying to get hold of her by daily calling on her, but was conveniently blocked by her mother who had received instructions from her daughter who was just as insistent that she would not see him.

Now here he was walking towards her. She decided to be nice to him and accepted his invitation to accompany him on the bench overlooking the sea. Somehow he looked different not just because he had grown up to be a handsome man, but because he was looking remarkably clean and sobre. She glanced down at the ugly scar etched into his arm, an accident that had occurred when he was a child. She had never noticed it before, but while travelling on the ship, someone with a scar on the arm, kept recurring in her dreams, she could not put a face to it, until now. Why would that be important anyway?

It had always been so hard to have a conversation with him, because he was always stoned.

Feeling awkward she offered him a cigarette. He declined it and to her surprise he initiated the conversation.

'Isabelle and Mick are back from Jeffries bay' He knew June was interested in his sister's whereabouts.

'They have become Christians' he continued. June was not sure what that entailed, so she replied brightly.

'Yes, I'm a Christian too.' And took another pull on her cigarette.

At this reply, Ken burst out laughing.

'You,.... you're not a Christian..... how can you say that when you are into the occult?.... you can't be a Christian and be into the Occult!.'

Oh but I am....I have a picture of Christ on my wall when I tell people's fortunes' June suddenly remembered why she didn't want to talk to this difficult person. When he did speak he always had something contrary to say. The only recollection she had of him even showing a glimmer of interest in Christianity was at the Coffee bar all those years ago, when they had playfully entered the main church building and pretended to get married. That was the last time that Ken ever ventured inside a church. So what did he know about Christianity? Thought June. Yes, she was more of a Christian than his sister or him...why was he being all self righteous anyway? The best thing would be to 'split' as soon as possible, she thought, so she got to her feet. He followed suit. It wasn't going to be that easy to shake him off.

'Well, I'll be on my way now, cheers!' she said heartily, waving her hand like a wand as if he would disappear. Ken did not seem to take the hint and walked by her side. A white calico bag hung across his shoulder, it looked quite heavy and June wondered what in the world he was carrying?

'Jesu Tande wena Baba' He drawled as he swiftly pulled a Gospel tract out of his overloaded calico bag and insisted that an African passerby have it.

'Ya bo' came the response as the unsuspecting man laughed heartily at Ken's pathetic effort at the Zulu language.

June looked at him suspiciously, and decided to walk on ahead of him. He effortlessly caught up with her and launched into a nostalgic narrative. His words were tumbling over each other as he described his experience of finding Jesus. He recalled his sister's reaction when he told her to stop preaching to him.

'she commanded the demon to come out of me!' He said.

There was a tremor in his voice and he continued, 'Suddenly I felt really different....as if something dark had lifted from me.'

He turned to look at June, his expression was intense and serious.

'Now I have no desire to get high, or to even smoke cigarettes.'

His face suddenly looked as winsome as a child's.' Could June really be hearing such awesome words! Was it possible that change could take place so quickly in a person? She wished that it was true. She had to admit that he was behaving totally out of character.

So, all differences aside, she invited him up for a cup of tea. He sat on the edge of her bed and inspected her books, while she went to the kitchen. Boldly, he began to pull each one out of the book case and pile them precariously on top of each other.

He then presented June with the large pile , and without even a hint of tactfulness, he announced 'All these books should be burned.....'

June stood aghast, tea in hand. She could not believe that he had the audacity to condemn her

178

precious books in that way. She put the mug down and steered him to the door and closed it in his face.

Suddenly she wanted her mum.
'I am a Christian aren't I mum?'
she said that evening, as she lay in her bed.
'Of course you are darling!'
came the speedy answer as mother went to open the window for some fresh air. Suddenly a gust of wind swept into the room with such force that the curtain swirled around her mother and entangled her so completely that all that could be seen was her arms flaying around frantically. In the next instance, she was fighting to close the window again, which had nearly come off its hinges, it seemed. At the backdrop of the whistling wind and a little worse for wear she soldiered on with her speech. Her dishevelled, curly, red hair, adding to the effect of what she had to say to her daughter.

'Of course you are darling' she said again, 'you *are* a Christian....you're a lovely girl....now don't you worry about a single thing.' She smothered June with kisses, turned off the light and traipsed out of the room. The scent of her perfume trailed behind her and June suddenly felt a bit intoxicated by it all . Her mother had such strong convictions about her.

'My mum really fights in my corner,' thought June, as she felt an overwhelming desire to giggle at the recollection of her mother passionately fighting with the curtains. She could trust her mother to give her the answers she wanted to hear, and even the sound of the howling wind did not seem threatening anymore.

***

The cold shoulder that Ken received from June only made him more determined to prove his point, so, relentlessly he called at her door daily and just as relentlessly June refused to see him. His goal was to take her to the church that his sister and her boyfriend had introduced him to.

Eventually his persistent rapping at the door paid off and she was dragged off to church with him.

CHAPTER 28

'I can see clearly now the rain has come,
I can see all the obstacles in my way,
Its going to be a bright... bright.... bright sun shining
day.'
Jimmy Nash 1972

'I make no apologies for what I am going to say tonight' bellowed the short preacher with the Elvis Presley hairstyle. June had been slouching in her seat with her head on Ken's shoulder, chewing gum, but at this bold remark she sat upright, his authoritative tone was more than slightly foreboding.

A story of Jesus from the Gospels was brought to life and given personal meaning to everyone sitting there. At the end of the message the pastor gave an invitation for those who did not know Christ to come to the front of the church and receive Him as Saviour and Lord.

June felt quite content with the commitment that she had made all those years ago at the holiday camp, so she slid back in her chair, and chewed her gum contentedly again, as she laid her head back on Ken's shoulder. Suddenly, she felt three pairs of eyes staring intensely at her. Isabelle, Mick and Ken were determined to see her at the front of the church. She shuffled around on her chair uneasily until she stumbled out of her seat and made her way to the front of the church with many other people.

It was the next day that she felt the implications of what she had done. She reached for a cigarette and suddenly became aware that the desire to smoke had left her. At that point she realized that something real was happening inside of her. Many times before she had tried to give up smoking, even substituting them with cream cakes, but she had failed hopelessly to get rid of the craving for tobacco. But now, suddenly feeling very tired, she placed the packet back on the shelf and curled up on the bed, and fell fast asleep.

There were only short intervals where she awoke from a marathon three day sleep in. Eventually her mother's insistent nagging jolted her out of unconsciousness.

'You can't sleep your whole life away!' she hollered and bundled June into the car, for a day out visiting family friends. Once more, June nodded off but was disturbed by a siren going past. She winced and glanced out of the window as words grafitteed on a building sped past her

'Jesus loves you. Give your life to Him!'. They read in bold letters. The words invoked the memory of what she had done those few days ago. She pondered on the decision she had made, she felt like a little child again. Reluctantly, she opened her heavy eyes. The sky suddenly seemed bluer and the air lighter. A sense of awe overcame her as she stepped out of the car to look at God's creation. It had been raining and now the sun was shining, everything sparkled and smelt of wet earth. It was as if all things had become new and washed clean. The impression was a feast for her senses and yet it was more than just and outward sensation, it was something that seemed to seep deep within the very core of her being.

The feeling of euphoria lingered with her and as the days went by the sleepiness gave way to hunger, a spiritual hunger for God's Word. The Bible which she had been given years before at the holiday camp, where she accepted Christ, became the centre of attention. It

182

was only logical to start from the beginning of the book, and she grew more and more awe struck with God's nature as she waded through the book of Genesis. For the first time, she could understand the message. It was as if a veil had been removed from her mind and spirit. God seemed to be speaking directly to her and her alone. This great Creator God seemed to be drawing uncannily close to her, to the point where she could, with conviction call him Father.

What followed was a discomforting feeling of unworthiness, which left June on her knees in prayer, repenting and weeping. This grew more extreme every time June attended church, because it was there that she learned of the Father's great gift to the world. Did He not send His unique and precious Son to suffer and die for her? The more she thought on these things, the more she wanted to please him and surrender her life to him.

The sense of unworthiness eventually, gave way to a profound awareness of her self worth in the sight of God. She realized how precious she was to Him. How awesome it was to realize that if she were the only person on earth, Jesus would still have come down to earth to save her. This was the greatest love story ever!

No longer did she hate herself or feel that she didn't make the mark. How could she hate herself when God loved her so much?

It was during one of these times of reflection and self examination, that she became aware of the literature that was in her book case. No longer was it Ken dictating to her what she should do with her life, but it was the gentle voice of the Holy Spirit who directed her to release her hold on the literature that had long formed her ideas. After some time of struggle, her books, tarot cards and occultic jewellery was disposed of. She dusted the book case with care and with deliberation placed her Bible, lovingly, onto one of the bare shelves.

* * *

One of the great drawing cards to the church had been the quality of the music that was enjoyed by the congregation. The hymns and songs were sung with great gusto. If there was a true picture of what it was to worship God, she had experienced it there.

This made her look again at the music that she had been listening to and suddenly the whole neighbourhood heard the news that June was giving away her LPs.... first come first serve. Friends that she hadn't seen for ages appeared on her doorstep to see what she was throwing away and soon news got around that June had 'got religion'.

Some of June's friends were genuinely impressed at what had happened to her and showed an interest in following the same path, but most of them frittered away and never crossed over the threshold of her place again, but however they responded did not concern the new convert, as she was just so delighted to have been released from the social trappings of the drug culture. She realized that this was the only way she could truly escape from the snare that she had been progressively falling into.

CHAPTER 29

'I want to see the light
So deep within you.   Moody Blues 1969

It was during this time that her parents were becoming a bit worried at the turn of events in June's life. They were hoping it was just another fad that would soon fade away. But as the weeks went on, it became more and more evident that her new life style was there to stay.

'So what's next on the agenda? Her mother asked, one day, 'Are you going to become a nun?'

June looked at her strangely and said

'no?!'

It all came to a head one evening when June came plunging through the front door exclaiming that she was nearly killed by a speeding car, that appeared 'out of nowhere' as she described it. She was very alarmed and genuinely distressed at what had happened. Feeling the weight of spiritual opposition, she began to cry.

This was all too much for her dad, who had been listening, unbelievably to her story as she stumbled over her words.

'You talk about the devil....it's you that has the devil!'

he shouted and strided into the bedroom slamming the door behind him. June was surprised at her Dad's reaction, It had jolted her out of her selfindulgence and she wiped her eyes in bewilderment wondering what was going on. It was totally out of character for him to express himself so angrily.

She straddled through to her room and sat on the edge of her bed looking up at the ceiling. Suddenly she was consumed by a terrible fear that she would be alone and that her parents would reject her because of her new found faith. She felt an eerie presence the same presence that she believed had tried to kill her earlier on in the evening. She trembled at the thought of it. If only her parents could understand what had happened to her, although to tell the truth, she could not understand herself. All she knew was that God loved her and Jesus was truly in her heart.

The fear continued to rise within her, like an icy finger creeping up her spine. Tears sprang to her eyes and dark thoughts sped through her mind.

'Oh God, please don't let my dad reject me!' she cried in desperation. Her heart began to beat rapidly and her breathing became heavy. These feelings were new to her. She had experienced a sense of loneliness before, but this brand of loneliness was much more profound. It seemed so complete, so final. She looked up at the lamp. A fly was buzzing frantically around it. It needed to be let out of the window, but she couldn't raise herself to the task.

Apart from the buzzing, quietness loomed. She took a deep breath and closed her eyes. The cold finger of fear had at last ebbed away and in its place, peace like soothing warm oil seeped over her soul..

She winced suddenly, for she heard a voice, deep within her. It was calm and gentle, not like the voices that had bellowed at her since adolescence, this voice stirred her as far back as infancy. She knew it was He who had counted her every heartbeat, since birth, who was speaking......He said,

'*I* am your Father, and *I* will never leave you.'

She shivered with shock at the heavenly encounter and awareness of her new found courage, erased every trace of fear. Everything would be ok.....

***

'Do you want me to pack up and leave?' she eventually said to her mother, as she made for the sofa and sat on the edge of it, feeling a bit like a stranger in her own home.

'No, no dear, we just want what's best for you. It's true though, there has been a remarkable change in you but it's all been so quick and out of the blue.' Mother's voice thinned to a whisper . She sat down next to her daughter and placed her arm around her quivering shoulders.

June could have refuted that it had come out of the blue, for many months she had been at her wits end, hardly leaving her room, for days. Mentally she had found life too hard to bare. She shifted around on the sofa moving her skirt awkwardly over her legs. She looked down at her bare fingers that were, just a few weeks ago, decorated with rings. That was not the only part of her body that was now bare from ornament. Her face was visibly lacking the usual attention that it used to receive. It was now pale and fragile, and free from any cosmetics. Yet the touch of other worldliness that it now possessed, was curiously attractive, in an innocent sort of way.

'Anyway what do you want for your eighteenth birthday?' Mother continued cheerily, trying to change the subject. June thought for a moment and then without any more hesitation, answered.

'I would like you to come to church with me......that's what I want for my birthday.'

*   *   *

It was on June's eighteenth birthday at church, that her mother experienced a complete turn around in her life. She had always been quite pious, but after taking the same path that June did, by surrendering her life to Christ, she discovered a new freedom that could not be described. Her conversion was just about as dramatic as her daughter's.

Instead of enjoying a cigarette together, they now sat around the Bible discussing texts and she was happy to open up her home to all the young people in the neighbourhood who were curious to know more of their new found faith.

On one of these evenings June's mother admitted that she thought that June had lost her mind, especially when she locked herself in her room and began to pray in a strange language. She then confessed that one night she had overheard June repeating the word 'Thankyou' in pure, clear Arabic. Having been born in the Sudan she was familiar with the language. It was this particular occasion that made her think that, perhaps there was something in all this 'hocus pocus' after all.

Then one evening June's dad was jolted out of his dark broodings and feelings of abandonment, by a surprise visit from an English gentleman who attended the parish church, he begrudgingly listened to the simple message of the Gospel. Being outnumbered by the women in his life, he put up the white flag and gave his heart to Jesus. June suspected that the English gentleman had been sent over by the pretty lady and her husband, who had led the Coffee bar, and comforted the grieving couple, those many months before. A friendship developed between the two men and they became inseparable in their holy exploits to reach their community with the Gospel.

***

Ken, on the other hand was not faring so well, and had found himself in prison after snatching an old lady's bag. He was getting frequent visits from his sister.
June found it hard to understand how he could vacillate from one extreme to the other. Had he not been the one who was so keen to see a change in her? Yet, here he was behaving badly once again.

One day, she accompanied Isabelle and Mick to the cells. Out of the darkness emerged a shirtless figure clad in white jeans.

189

'I've promised God that if He gets me out of this fix, I will serve him forever,' Ken said decisively as he held his sister's serious gaze.

Mick approached him and placed his hand on his shoulder. 'Brother, Satan has lost this battle for your soul, Jesus has a great purpose for your life. Do you believe this?'

Tears came to Ken's eyes. He had always seemed so remote, and yet there he was showing some emotion. Emotions that had been repressed since he was a child.

God, it seemed and, of course, the old lady who had her bag snatched, looked kindly on Ken's plight, and he was swiftly released from prison to prove himself.

As well as heaven looking graciously upon him, the military had their eyes on him as well. Somehow they had caught up with him.

His call up papers had arrived at his sister's new address. They, being, just a few months ago, fully fledged hippies, had given up their travels around the Wild Coast and instead opted for a studio flat on the South Beach. No furniture had been donated to them, but they were happy sleeping on the floor and drinking out of one mug while listening to sermons on their small cassette player. Soon a small group of friends, including June and Ken, met together, at the little flat to have bible studies and discussions.

One evening, out of the blue, Bobby appeared at the door clutching a new bible close to his heart. June could not hide her surprise. He sat down beside her and with his yellow pipe stained fingers, reverently paged through the Gospels. He shared that it was while sitting in the military prison that Jesus appeared to him, after he was given a New Testament which confirmed that his experience was true.

Although only a small lamp lit the room, there was a brightness energised and charged by God's presence, as each girl and boy shared their story of their encounter with Jesus.

In the half light, June recognized Robbie and recalled, silently to herself, the day that she noticed him, as he sat in his combie van, looking at the surf. She remembered the anger and pain in his eyes as she attempted to approach him. But now, his face showed no signs of the former destructive emotions. The shadows from the lamp only highlighted the expression of joy that danced across his furrowed brow.

His journey to Christ had been a hard struggle. Several times he and his brothers had endured shock treatment in the psychiatric hospital, which was an ominous institution out in the hills. According to the medical staff, this was the answer to the problems of people that had drug induced psychosis. Robbie's mother, being a nurse, naturally agreed with the decision and rounded her sons up regularly, sending them off to hospital to get sorted out. What more could be done for her hallucinogenic, hungry boys?....nothing.

In the mental health world, there was not much else.

Apart from his mental health issues Robbie had still managed to win surfing championship status but his struggles with psychotic attacks still continued to harass him relentlessly.

'I was a very angry man' he confessed as he fumbled with the pages of his Bible. 'but now I have this overwhelming peace, which passes all understanding...' His voice broke and he was close to tears. His whole demeanour had changed to one of meekness and humility, the complete opposite to his former self.

At this, June was overwhelmed with the reality that her friends had been truly transformed by the power of Jesus.

***

Basking in the blissful sunshine of the nearness of God's presence, was something that June thought would go on forever, but she and her friends, soon learned that there was a spiritual enemy, a force to be reckoned with, that was not going to go away without an ongoing battle.

June became very conscious of this opposing force, when Jimmy made his way back to her front door.

'I received a letter from you and I thought you had gone mad' he explained as he sat on the couch looking handsome. 'It wasn't just because you had found religion, but it was your writing it was slanting steeply down the page.....'

June giggled...yes it was true when she got excited she always tended to slide her writing down the page, taking no heed to straight lines. It must've looked a little crazy she agreed, but then Jimmy was crazy. It was remarkable that he had even attempted to verbalize his thoughts to her. He seemed strangely attentive.

Feeling that this was a sign from God, she launched into a rhetorical account of her experience of finding Christ and then waited for his response. She joined him on the couch and asked if she could pray for him, impulsively laying her hand on his shoulder and praying vocally. [xlii]Her requests to God became more assertive as they followed the direction of verbal confrontation with demon powers, which she rebuked in Jimmy's ear.

Suddenly to her surprise, he interrupted what she was saying. His face was still bowed and expressionless, his lips did not move, and yet a deep, vicious voice emerged from his throat.

'You have no power over me....you have No authority over ME...who do you think you are?'

the accusation had a threatening ring to it. It was too eerie for June and shook her to the core.

'But I do...I say I do?' she stammered in a thin voice and placed her trembling hand timidly back in her lap, waiting for him to open his eyes.

Jimmy turned his face to look at her, his expression was emotionless. She tried to compose herself, hoping that she had succeeded in concealing her shock, and then without any hesitation, he said

'June.....what you have.......I am going to run from forever.' He stood up resolutely, reached out for his kit bag and withdrew from her home for the last time.

CHAPTER 30

And it seems like and it feels like
And it seems like yes it feels like
A brand new day, yeah
A brand new day!
Van Morrison 1970

Ken had been called up to the infantry. Predictably, like many that had gone before him, he determined to run from his fate. He was incensed with the thought of spending a whole year in the army.

'Maybe this is what God wants for your life...perhaps it will keep you on the straight and narrow.' June said, reflectively, one day, when he was particularly disgruntled.

'There is no way I am going to carry a rifle.' He replied gruffly.

'Well, perhaps you won't have to carry a rifle...just go to the army, you might even like it.' She answered persistently, not believing a word that she, herself was saying, but smiling reassuringly at him.

The suggestion must have worked because he eventually presented himself to the military before they arrested him.

True to his word, he refused to carry a rifle, and to exasperate the 'powers that be' even more he refused to stand at attention when his superiors entered the barracks.....his excuse was that he was reading the Bible. There was nothing that the authorities could do with him, because he was clearly, reading his bible. What they could do though, was transfer him.

Hence he was moved to another section of the army. The 'Medics' a department where they were not trained to fight but rather to save lives.. He was placed in a Durban hospital close to June's home and in the evenings he would visit June and eat dinner with her family. More and more people from the community felt welcome to join the family at the table, and soon June's mother was dishing up for many of the lonely and poor in the neighbourhood. When June's dad was at the table, he would break bread before the meal and all those present were compelled to remember the drama that unfolded when the Lord broke bread for the last time with his disciples.

***

It was one of those Kodak moments for June, who, at the click of the camera, contrived a plan to keep Rab away. Rab had promised undying love to June and corresponded faithfully, letting her know that he was on his way to confirm the engagement to her, as soon as he could get work on the next sea faring vessel that would have him. So, clad in an extra large rugby jersey with her hair pulled back in a tight bun, she smiled a cheesy grin into the lense. Her mother was in on the conspiracy and smiled impishly as she presented her daughter to the fiancé to be. The daft picture did the trick and Rab literally disappeared off the face of the earth.

June was clearly 'burning all her bridges behind her, and making it as hard as possible to find the trail back to her old life, even to the point of repelling most of the friends of her youth, in the process. She didn't seem to care that she was being totally reckless in her awkward extravagance towards her new found faith in God. There was a lot of zeal in her pursuit for holiness, but not much wisdom. Irrespective of this, there was a feeling within her that she was growing to love her fellow man more than ever. Something extraordinary seemed to be taking place within her, it was as if she was growing 'spiritual muscles'.

Like a bomb that was ready to detonate, Rachel, became the first recipient to this clumsy display of explosive love. June had become estranged from her long time school friend when their relationship fermented into a cauldron of competiveness and jealousy. With jaded cynicism, June had come to the conclusion that Jewish people were best left alone. Her view had progressively formed into a notion that said ... Jews and Gentiles were fundamentally different and never the two should meet. But now things had changed, she only felt love for those who were different from her.

On this particular night, June had captured her little, old time friend on the streets and had hugged her to the point where Rachel had to struggle to get free from her embrace.

***

The overwhelming love she had for Rachel and her kin, compelled her to visit Rachel's home one evening.
'Sorry to just rock up like this without letting you know.' She said, hoping that she would be welcomed inside. The family was aware that June had become overwhelmed with her new found faith and were reluctant to let her in, but couldn't just leave her at the door.

'Yeh sure, come in' Rachel replied weakly and left the door opened for June to enter as she disappeared into adjoining room.

June capered haltingly into the dining room where Rachel's dad was sitting forlornly and alone at the carefully set table. The television was on in the background.

It was a Friday night, the Sabbath. The candles had not been lit. In better times he would have had his family sitting around the table with him, but after the tragic death of his son, his family had lost their fervour for faith and tradition. Rachel's disillusionment at the death of her big brother had been complete, causing her to leave her Jewish roots altogether and at about the same time that June became a Christian, Rachel found solace in Eastern mysticism and the New Age movement. She had become an avid follower of such and found it hard to connect with her former best friend.

Eventually she appeared from her bedroom. She had grown into an elegant young lady and she sat gracefully down opposite June. June thought for a moment on what to say. Seeing that their worlds had become so distant from each other, it was hard to find common ground.

'Have you heard from Irene, lately?' June inquired, invoking some sort of conversation. Irene had been a mutual friend to them both.

'Well no, not lately' came the reply as Rachel poured the wine and her mother brought in the bread.

After Irene's sadness of losing her Asian boyfriend in a car accident she had found comfort in a lesbian relationship.

'I saw her in town and she is like a new person' continued June. Rachel raised her well shaped eyebrows and twirled her wine glass around on the pure white table cloth, looking inquiringly at June. June took this as a signal to continue.

'well, yes.. she shared that she had a dream. Jesus stood before her and told her to follow Him....so that's what she has done...she's following Him.'
June shrugged and smiled vacantly, and added
' There's been a remarkable change in her.'

There was a tremor from Rachel's dad. It occurred that she was not only oblivious to the fact that she was sitting in Elijah's chair, the chair that by tradition, was left empty for the coming Messiah, but she was also talking about the imposter Jesus at the Sabbath meal. How much more could he tolerate?

Rachel's face remained expressionless, but she was curious to see what her dad's reaction would be. To her surprise, he sighed deeply and then responded by asking June a question.

'So this Jesus....what is it that all you young people are raving about at present?

'It's easy....June answered,

'Just as the angel of death would not enter into the homes of those who had marked their door posts with the blood of the lamb, but passed over them, so the blood of Jesus, when he died on the cross, has made it possible for us to overcome death....if we believe in Him...you see he rose again...He is the Passover lamb....that which you are celebrating tonight.'

June had incapsulated the whole message of the Bible in a single breath and had alluded to the book of Exodus in the Torah.

There was a poignant moment where all that could be heard was the sound of the television in the background. Rachel arose from her chair and disappeared into the bedroom. Her dad fiddled with the silverware on the table and looked intently at June. He picked up the bread and began to break it slowly and thoughtfully. Clear audible words, unexpectedly drifted over from the Television set.

'Just as God used Moses to set His people free from slavery, so, Jesus has come to set us free from the slavery of sin'.

June looked at the television screen, there was a pastor sharing the gospel message. The Jewish man at the head of the table looked intently at June for a moment. They were both aware that the message that was coming from the television set was confirming what June had just said. The atmosphere became intense, so intense that no-one knew what to do. Rachel did not appear again from her room.

'I guess I better be going' stammered June, as she arose and slung her bag over her shoulders. She glanced back to see the lonely man deep in thought, but was led promptly out through the front door by his protective wife.

It was a few weeks later that Rachel's dad died, unexpectedly and June hoped that he had heeded the call to accept his Messiah.

[xliii]Her love for the Jewish people continued to grow, as she realized that they were the ones through whom God gave the Holy Scriptures and the Saviour of the world.

***

The congregation sang from their hearts and worshipped with fervour. June turned to Kenny, her handsome boyfriend. He was deep in prayer. They were in the midst of people of all races. Even though the Apartheid was at its peak in power, it could not restrain people from all walks of life, coming together with one thing in common...to worship God.

In front of her, stood her friend, Buzz, less his little dog 'Cat'. He was happy and free. . she was overwhelmed with joy at the thought, that her friends and family were a part of this exuberant celebration.

June pondered on the definition of the church.

'what is it?' she wondered,

'It is a diverse company of people from every race, where there is no class distinction, where political and cultural differences dissolve in the radiant light of Christ. It is in this life giving knowledge that unity is created'

And there was nothing that the government could do about that.....they could not refute that truth!'

'All those who need healing come now and let us pray!' declared the preacher with conviction, as he called from the pulpit. Many people rose from their chairs and made their way to the front of the church. June joined the many. After all, when she was twelve, she had injured her back when sliding down a sand dune.

A WORD FROM THE AUTHOR.

The reason I have written this story is to try and address my daughter's pressing question of how I could have lived under such a government and not do anything about it?'

For a long time I shrugged the question aside, until at last I felt it necessary to confront the issues of my youth.

I hope that as you read this coming of age story, you will be able to feel the heart beat of the youngsters that were caught in the conundrum of the age.

It was the late 60's and early 70's. The cold war was raging and was a convenient launching pad for the ideas of apartheid, which found fertile ground in South African politics .

The racist ideology had officially become the law of the land in 1948 , and consequently, caused the country to be excluded from the global community. This affected South Africans as a whole, some more than others.

Although it looked like the white youth were apathetic and indifferent to the situation in the country, there brewed, not only a visible war which expressed itself through compulsory military call ups, for all those of a white skin, but also an invisible war, which unfolded in the ethos of the age, via the drug culture. This lethal mixture of the drug culture and cruel politics spawned the need within the hearts of this little group of friends to search for meaning and forgiveness.

As I have spent time writing this story, it has helped me to get a grip on my personal history. It has given me the chance to be a little more lenient on myself. I hope that as you read the story of a young girl who was a bit dazed and confused, it will give you a different take on some of the white youth in that little corner of the Republic, during the apartheid years. I hope it will soften your outlook slightly.

On behalf of myself and my peers I would also like to say sorry to all those who suffered so terribly during the apartheid years.

My second reason for writing this story is to warn young people of the dual danger of getting involved, or even dabbling in the occult with the use of drugs as a vehicle to open the door to the dark side.

My own story ends on a triumphant note, but I must confess that my Christian walk has not been an easy one. It has been full of tragedy and pain. I feel that the folly of my youth and the dabbling with hallucinogenics as a doorway into the occult, have attributed to many of the unfortunate things that have happened to me.

Therefore I would advise everyone who has taken the time to wade through my modest testimony to avoid such activities at all costs. Even as it is clearly stated in Deuteronomy 18, 8 -12

When you come into the land which the Lord your God gives you, you shall not learn to follow the abominable practices of these nations. There shall not be found among you anyone who makes his son or daughter pass through the fire, or who uses divination, or is a soothsayer, or an augur, or a sorcerer, or a charmer, or a medium or a wizard, or a necromancer.............................'

I do not refute the fact that in these dangerous days, it is becoming increasingly difficult to decipher between what is harmless and what is not, especially since the dark arts are glamorised and promoted by the media.. My prayer is that this generation will have wise discernment to know the difference.

Lastly, I have written this story, in memory of my amazing Mum and Dad. A mother who threw herself at the mercy of God in prayer, only to see God give her the requests of her heart, and a father who was humble enough to see the error of his ways and do a complete U turn to follow in the footsteps of Christ. Such examples encourage parents everywhere and emphasise the value that God puts on the family unit and the desire He has to see entire families enter the joy of the Kingdom of God.

CHAPTER 2
[i] Kenyatta was arrested in 1952, being charged as a member of the Mau Mau, a radical anti-colonial movement, engaged in rebellion against Kenya's British rule. In 1962 he was elected as president of the country.(Wikipedia)

CHAPTER 4
[ii] Africans working in the cities were subject to curfew regulations and pass book requirements. If they could not produce a pass they were subject to arrest. Such permits did not include the spouse and family of the permit holder, contributing to the breakup of family life among many Africans.
(www. encyclopedia/apartheidhtml)

CHAPTER 5
[iii] There is a prayer that initiates a relationship with Jesus Christ. It is based on the scripture in Revelation 3,20, where Jesus says:
'Behold, I stand at the door and knock, if anyone hears my voice and opens the door, I will come in to him and dine with him and he with Me.'

[iv] A tug is a small but powerfully engined motor boat that pulls the big ships into harbour. A 'tug hand' is a crew member.

CHAPTER 7
[v] There are three levels of traditional healing. The *Inyanga* is the herbalist and is concerned with medicines made from animals and plants. The *isangoma*, makes contact with the ancestral spirits and prescribes medicine according to their dictates. The *Isanusi* is a diviner who detects sorcerers and other so called evil doers. Many of them operate from their own shops in the back streets of Durban.

CHAPTER 8

[vii] Nelson Mandela rose to prominence in the African National Congress in 1952. Working as a lawyer, he was repeatedly arrested for seditious activities. In 1962 he was arrested and convicted for saboutage and conspiracy to overthrow the government. He was sentenced to life imprisonment. (Wikipedia)

[viii] *"The security and happiness of all minority groups in South Africa depends on the Afrikaner."*
President PW Botha, as quoted in *Dictionary of South African Quotations*, Jennifer Crwys-Williams, Penguin Books 1994, p11.

[ix] The SACC (South African Council of Churches) led by the Archbishop, Bill Burnett incurred the state's wrath by publishing the *Message to the people of South Africa* in 1968. By the 1970's they were supporting liberation organisations, through programmes to combat racism which led to debate on violence and liberation. (*The Church Struggle in South Africa* by J.W. de Gruchy and S. de Gruchy*)*

CHAPTER 9

[ix] *Rhodesian bush war* or the *War of liberation*, was a civil war between 1964-1979. The conflict pitted three forces against each other. The Rhodesian government under Ian Smith, the *Zimbabwe African National Liberation Army* led by Robert Mugabe, and the *Zimbabwean People's Revolutionary Army* of Joshua Nkomo. 1979 saw the end of white minority rule. (Wikipedia)

[x] Roger Daltrey, founder and vocalist of the British band the 'Who' known for his beautiful blond curls. In the 70's

CHAPTER 11

[x] The Sharpsville Massacre took place outside the police station in the Transvaal in 1960. After a day of demonstrations, the crowd far outnumbered the police, hence, they opened fire on the crowd and consequently killed 69 people.

CHAPTER 9

[xi] SA was invited to the 1968 games in Mexico, but this elicited such sharp protests from Black African countries, who threatened to withdraw if SA participated, that the IOC was obliged to withdraw its invitation in April, 1969.
Liebenberg, B.J. & Spies, S.B. (eds)(1993). *South Africa in the 20th Century, Pretoria:* Van Schaik Academic, pp. 431 & 432.

CHAPTER 13

[xiii] Thankyou
[xiv] A Sjambok is a long, heavy leather whip. Typically South African.
[xv] 'I love you great God' In Zulu.

CHAPTER 14

[xvi] *Vasbyt* ' bite hard' a bit like the English 'stiff upper lip'

[xvii] *Larnie* somebody who is officially in authority. Or 'posh'
[xviii] *Speel* 'play'
[xix] The nation called the *Coloureds,* the Asians and the Black people were exempt from the army and were not allowed to own arms of any sort. It was compulsory that white South Africans gave up to 2 years of their lives in the army and after that they had to attend army camps until they were over a certain age. Only white South Africans could own a gun.
[xx] *Awol* 'run away'
[xxi] Jehovah Witnesses were passifists, thus, they were arrested and jailed for not adhering to the military call up.
[xxii] *Zol* 'Marijuana'
[xxiii] *Malpitte* The correct name is *Datura Stramonium* and is a powerful hallucinogen which produces intense visions. However the tripane alkaloids which are responsible for both the medicinal and hallucinogenic properties are fatally toxic in only slightly higher amounts than the medicinal dosage and careless use often results in hospitalization and deaths. W*ikipedia*
[xxiv] The front wheel lifting up as the bike takes off.'
[xxv] Marijuana cigarette.

CHAPTER 15
[xxvi] Parabats, Part of the South African Air force, parachutists.

CHAPTER 16
[xxvii] 1 Corinthians 10, 12

CHAPTER 17
[xxviii] The word *ducktail* originated from the 1950's, when it was the fashion for men to grease their hair back into what looked like a duck's tail
[xxix] Reveller
[xxx] 'He's in prison because he beat up an English man outside a Durban night club.'

CHAPTER 18
[xxxi] Timothy Leary was a 1960's counter culture icon, who wrote many books, including *The Psychedelic Experience*. He was a campaigner for psychedelic drugs research and use.

CHAPTER 22
[xxxii] Revelation 3.18 *'therefore I counsel you to purchase from Me gold refined and tested by fire, that you may be wealthy, and white clothes to clothe you and to keep the shame of you rnudity from being seen, and salve to put on your eyes that you may see.'*

[xxxiii] Electroconvulsive Therapy or electroshock, a psychiatric treatment in which seizures are electrically induced in anaesthetized patients for therapeutic effect
[xxxiv] Ouija board
[xxxv] **Nirvana** is achieved after a long process of committed application to the path of purification (Pali: Vissudhimagga) taught by the Buddha. (Wikipedia)
[xxxvi] Lobsang Rampa wrote *The Third Eye*. His real name was Cyril Henry Hoskin. He claimed to be a Tibetan Lama.
[xxxvii] The Third eye is the doorway to spiritual perception.

CHAPTER 24
[xxxviii] The Gospel of Matthew 7,7
[xxxix] John 14,6 *'I am the way the truth and the life, no man comes to the Father but by Me.'*

207

CHAPTER 25
[xl] *Dead Skunk* is a 1972 novelty song by Loudon Wainwright 111

CHAPTER 25

[xli] The **South African Border War**, commonly referred to as the **Angolan Bush War** in South Africa, was a conflict that took place from 1966 to 1989 largely in **South-West Africa** (now **Namibia**) and **Angola** between South Africa and its allied forces (mainly **UNITA**) on the one side and the Angolan government, **South-West Africa People's Organisation** (SWAPO), and their allies (mainly **Cuba**) on the other. It was closely intertwined with the **Angolan Civil War** and the **Namibian War of Independence** (Wikipedia)

CHAPTER 29
[xlii] Main line Pentecostals and Protestant Charismatics would not separate the duties of clergy and laity in the performance of exorcism. (*Int. Dict.of Pentecostal and Charismatic Movements* by S.Burgess ande.M. van der Maas. Zondervan.)

CHAPTER 30
[xliii] Romans 8, 1-5 *'To whom pertain the adoption, the glory, the covenants, the giving of the law, the service of God, and the promises: of whom are the fathers and from whom, according to the flesh, Christ came.'*